Not Accounted For

A brief collection of short stories and essays

by Gari Hart

Table of contents

Introduction by author..01

Estranged: pieces of fiction

    Her Tale Near Midnight..17

    House of Mirrors..27

    Yellow Roses..47

    The Turning Point...71

    BPM Counter..101

    Phantom Creatures in the Woods............................133

    Revolver Anatomy...157

    Psychogenic Stranger..187

    Out of Context...217

Rehabilitated: non-fiction

    I Want the Answers: the untold feminism of the

    X- Files..253

    Exploring the Reoccurring Reincarnation Theme in

    Wachowski Films..263

    For a More Just World: an interview with Director

    Kyzza Terrazas...277

Introduction

Although I knew it would not be easy, I honestly believed the process of pulling this collection together would go relatively quick. All the pieces were there, they only needed some retooling. I was not naive enough to think each story required merely a draft or two, but I certainly incorrectly estimated my ability to plow thru each draft. This was due in part to misgauging where I wanted to end up and the direction I was going to take to get there. If that makes any sense. Along the way to completing this project my inspirations matured or changed, and when you are at liberty to follow them, not being obliged to a deadline – or, let's face it, an audience – you're prone to free fall for a bit. Or, in my case, much too long. I have been known to remind friends you cannot plan for everything, and that advice came around to bite me from behind on the journey of this compilation.

Originally my intention was not to produce a collection of short and flash fictions; I had my sights focused on novels. As my first novel, *Concealed Weapons*, was failing to snare interest with literary agents, I moved straight into working on my second novel, *By the Somber Spectra of Microgravity*. Not long into that venture, I figured genuine feedback was essential in order to improve my craft. Friends and family can be supportive and wonderful, but fundamentally they are biased and typically will praise you in any case. For honest reflection and constructive criticism, you need strangers who might relentlessly tell the drawbacks (and the strengths) in your writing. And so I joined a local workshop group. Joining a workshop might sound like a no-brainer, but I have some issues working with people in-person, so it took me a while to make that leap. Though not a requirement at all, most members submitted short and flash pieces for review. I thought it would be a great exercise to try myself. I would not have guessed how it would lead me to discover and appreciate the art of presenting a story within a condensed frame. Creating shorts is more akin to photography: Zeroing-in on a single moment that will convey a comprehensive tale. After more than a year of participating in that workshop, I decided to try to self-publish a collection of short stories.

    Someone in the workshop verbalized my writing tends to have a common theme of alienation. Having a running or go-to theme does not bother me personally, so I thought it best to play on that. The central motif of this collection was intended to be an existential examination of alienation. Maybe it still is, if one wanted to argue. Over time the tone shifted around, and in effect the stories required revisions after revisions to better adhere to the inconstant nature of the book. Finally I decided these stories best fit a less sophisticated variation or exact definition of a theme: They are simply about people who have lost their guiding light. The road has gone dark, and they're too far from either the beginning or end to figure the best course.

There is a part of me disappointed that I could not make everything work the way it was originally envisioned. Eventually though, it became now or never. By continuing to hem and haw over syntax and bellyache about whether or not they fit, I inestimably postponed the finalization of what was supposed to be a rather uncomplicated process. I know some of these pieces could certainly go through another draft or two, and turn out in better condition. But in that scenario, A) the collection would never get done, B) Later works would potentially display no growth on my part as an author. Unquestionably I'm looking forward to readers, if any, being able to track my development in comparing future works.

Several pieces were cut from the final product. They either strayed too far from the theme or were taking too long to perfect. Included in the excerpts were three novelettes intended to be centerpieces for this collection.

Ironically, I felt they were among those which strayed too far; they were morphing into something else. As those were fleshed out, the stories grew more complex. All of the excluded pieces are stories I still believe in and hope to publish sometime in my life. Only time will tell though, I suppose. In life we conceive of so many plans, have grand intentions, but can only manage to get a lamentably small percentage of them accomplished. It seems to me that some people have gone, or went their entire existence only dreaming of, never actualizing their desires and plans.

  I cultivated this collection of fiction while working a "real" job, while writing other narratives, while composing two music projects, while planning a wedding, and while forging time to simply enjoy my life here and there. I worked hard, because I did not want be someone who said but never did.

Before even starting this project, I moonlighted as a film columnist for Examiner. Additionally, I published articles occasionally on various Chicago sites. The position at Examiner was fun, because it elevated to a degree where I qualified for press sites and credentials. This allowed for easier access to movies during events like the Chicago International Film Festival and Chicago Underground Film Festival, as well as free tickets to screenings for major studio releases. Over the course of putting this book together though, Examiner went under and my articles were deleted from the internet. Roughly a year after that, more sites where my work had been published vanished as well. There became a trend of all my work (not to mention the work of some other great unknown writers) being erased. And I won't lie, it was upsetting. However, as this project was wrapping up and some pieces were removed from the final product, I decided to include a few choice selections from my journalistic repertoire. Even though they do not fit the theme to any respect. One of the benefits of self-publishing a book however is the allowance to do whatever the Hell you want.

    It is hard to say what I learned from this experience overall. Everything that initially comes to mind I already knew. *Writing and self-publishing is hard work*: Duh! *You are your own toughest critic*: No shit. Looking back, this was the journey of me finding my voice, or written voice rather, and learning what kind of writer I am. What is my procedure? What is my focus? The thing I really feel learned is how capable I am of achieving goals. No matter how long the book seemed to be taking, and how many times I thought I could not continue, I took a few deep breaths, got up and proceeded with determination. True, writing something is not physically forbidding or challenging, so some people don't understand the problem, but there are equal amounts of mental roadblocks to overcome. There are still people rolling their eyes and not-so-secretly betting you won't see it through to the end. There is still a high level of self-motivation you must find. This experience has not only been beneficial for myself, but for the support and advice I can pass on to others. I'm looking forward to telling others working on projects to shut up and keep going.

So, what now? The end is never the end. This will not be the last time you hear from me. When working in any art medium, it's good practice to brainstorm your next project before finishing your present one. As you can guess though, after taking so long to finish this one, there is a backlog of ideas of which I've hardly scratched the surface. Choosing the next one is not a simple ask. Some much to do, so little time. I suppose I will not waste any more time writing this introduction then.

Onward.

Estranged

pieces of fiction

Her Tale Near Midnight

To her assumed peers she was merely a commoner. One hell bent on appearing cultured and educated, but nothing more. They appreciated the effort it must have took to penetrate their elevated social class, or to register on their radar for that matter, but they denied regarding her as an equal. This blue-collar woman, who taught herself three languages, trained in classical ballet, who had become well versed in the history of music and art, and who was as humbled as proud, they would never willingly afford her the degree of recognition which cleanses that collar a crisp white. Permitted rather than welcomed at the standard social events, other guests reacted to her attendance with an adoration kin to that of a prized pet. To acknowledge her as a compeer was, in the minds of most, to invite a complete upsetting of sociological structure.

Clarifying a determining element, she had not been born into riches. She had forged her way into high society, through laboring and a keen insight for industry. Rising up through the ranks of the workers, from the very bottom to the top and beyond. Her money was earned, crusted with the sweat of a hard day, and was in no way the product of "rightful" downflow from a legacy blood line. In short, she was new money. *Her footprint found in the mud once and now she trudged the filth all over their homes,* as some clever socialite phrased it. The dollars in her possession were perceived, by a majority of the stuffy and safely fastened upper class snobs, as dollars stolen; *id est,* what should have been dollars rotated back into *their* pockets, to afford *their* needs and desires. Despite the rash of rather unwarranted antipathy though, she was indeed tolerated. To dismiss her from their ranks outright, like a banshee whose very existence forewarns of demise, would be bad form, lest their natural dark and mucky selves be exposed. Instead, they greeted her with clinched teeth, choked down drinks and hors d'oeuvres beside her. All the while seething with rejection underneath the falsity.

    This clandestine hostility was not lost on her. She saw thru the façade of their dishonest smiles and other contorted expressions. She figured they all would unanimously sigh with relief if she were to miraculously dematerialize from their company. These parties, dinners, and galas she attended, all with cognizance of her reputed standing, she did so for a purpose. A purpose she did not make readily available to anyone: Defiance. Aware her very presence was a disturbing aberration to their sensibilities, with her impoverished past frequently whispered from one self-appointed magnifico to the next as "unfortunate," her insistence to repeatedly publicly stand equal with neither shame nor trepidation amid these would-be superordinate stiffs was a disguise. A mute declaration, that decency could be found in any class. Every soiree she could make it through with civility, insight, and charm was a step forward for her and a step backwards for them, pushing them further into a corner. Eventually one day, they would have no choice but to either accept her or show their true colors.

    She knew parading around these events, spewing some sociological manifesto, it would fall upon deaf ears.

Even if the monologs were well-rehearsed for maximum elegance. Few people cared much to hear her persuasions to begin with, never mind if she impaired each opportunity to speak-up by exuding reproach for the higher class. Actions, including subtle non-aggressive ones, spoke louder than words and could leave deeper impressions. They might work subconsciously for her benefit as well. So, she often made her point simply by showing up to a party, not looking or acting as though she were out of her league. She could talk the talk and walk the walk, as they used to say in her old public high school. Meanwhile, her urges to discuss separation of class and its counterproductive nature to prosperity and real humanity remained unspoken. For the time, it simply had to be kept in reserve; Certainly she would comment on the topic, if ever it came up naturally by someone else. She also considered that degree of confrontation might not be for her to breech at all, but a task for successors to brave. Someone for which she was now merely opening the door. The influence she effected night after night was indeed infinitesimal, but nevertheless was a consistent dent in the system everyone would have to acknowledge and deal with sooner or later. And once they finally accepted her, the door would widen enough for more of *her kind* to flow in, flooding the upper class until they were inseparable from the lower. Even though the objective would probably take the rest of her life, she guessed, her spirit was determined, her patience insurmountable. After all, at her core she was a laborer, and never shrunk down in the shadow of hard work.

At the end of each night out, having endured at least a dozen tedious conversations, which invariably centered on the subject of money no matter how the crowd tried to pitch and manipulate it, she returned home to a modest house. Located on the outskirts of the city, the address fell near exactly on that line dividing urban from suburban, straddling the flimsy partition keeping the assumed respectable citizens and the mocked apart. A spot where she could look back from within and keep her minded rooted. Before retiring to bed in a set of cotton pajamas – the same kind she had worn since childhood – she would step to her patio. Dressed in whatever extravagant outfit and jewelry still from that evening, with her hair styled in whatever fashionable way – feeling more like in costume than comfortable – she would light a cigarette. A seemingly inextinguishable bad habit, but one she came to find necessary to regain a center. The inhale and exhale of the smoke made her feel like her real self. She gazed at the city skyline from her backyard, inhaling smoke that reminded her everyone has faults to be overlooked. Faults were a human feature.

If she could only make everyone see their own, then she could help everyone look passed and move forward together.

House of Mirrors

"How could I put this into words?"

For Deana that question, which plagued her mind and soured her mood, was not a matter of selecting the correct nouns and adjectives to tag a comprehensible depiction onto an experience, but a question of what point there was for doing so. To apply a series of definitions that might, to a microscopic degree, translated this *event* into words for those too hesitant to find out for themselves, it seemed somehow profane. The "event" itself, as Deana had come to call the experience, transcended description, and would be disgraced by the muddy and finite interpretations words would restrain it to. Like an artist who might chuckle on the inside at the art critic that endeavors in vain to deduce the pure emotion in their work, Deana believed this feeling simply was not of the same realm where words are employed. She felt a flood of satisfaction from knowing the ineffable, and let that experience whitewash and extenuate all her senses. In this single moment, there were no inane attachments, which typically clutched onto day to day moments desperately for life. Time and all its myriad of insurmountable drawbacks existed far off in another place that never existed, as if it were a nightmare Deana hoped to never revisit. This place, this "event" instead was the void of sensation and meaning, of obligation and compensation, and was a cyclic system of unrestrained serenity. Here, for what time she was there, Deana could believe her real life was only a bad dream. She would stay there in that cloud which knows of no discomfort indefinitely, if fortune may allow.

As it came to pass every time though, the haze of the event lost its integrity faster than it came. Deana could sense the nightmare of reality expanding in shape and intensity once again, and it felt like the sun was setting forever. Faces and objects from around the room started to bleed through her perfect cloud of denial, piercing the panoramic oblivion she managed to hide away in for a short while. Feelings, physical and emotional, fired up through her body. All the aches in the bones and muscle of her wretched form, etched in by years of excessive use pulled her back down from the high. And finally, awareness; the fervid discomfort of knowing reality. Deana was relatively cognizant of her actual surroundings now.

    The shabby couch she was slumped down on smelled worse than it looked, and it even hurt to sit upon. With random trash littering the gunky wood floors on the room around it though, the couch was the better option to collapse on once the effects of the drugs would kick in. Due to the absence of any sort of heat source, combined with the late fall weather outside, it was freezing in the room; Deana remembered walking through dead, wet leaves on her way there earlier. Whether the lamps propped on the floor were naturally too bright, or if the blaring light was another unfortunate aftereffect, she did not know, but regardless her eyes stung. With how little she could lift open her eyelids, everything she saw looked disheveled. The walls were dilapidated and covered with offensive graffiti, sprayed by deviant addicts with too much time on their hands and only one thing on their minds. The only clean area in the room was a corner where an accent table used to stand, purposed as a resting spot for the few porcelain pipes from which they all smoked - the table had been hocked a few days earlier to help pay for more drugs, and that corner had since remained ironically clear of the debris, and the pipes now rested wherever they fell.

    Deana suddenly noticed a young girl passed out next to her on the couch. Her legs curled up beside Deana, and her head fallen against the arm rest. From the look of her fashionable, unpolluted clothes and smooth face, Deana guessed she was new to the scene. The ravages of this lifestyle had not yet begun their outward spread. The girl looked too young to even be into weed, Deana thought, let alone something much stronger. This room was for heavy users, addicts who would get their fix anywhere and anyway they needed to, and losers who were compelled to perpetually push on to the next more potent thing to escape. Deana had started coming to this place for what her dealer called "cosmic dust." It was a new blend of DMT and some opioid, which nearly knocked you straight out into oblivion for approximately forty-five minutes. Cosmic dust was new, extremely potent and highly addictive. Which was how Deana found herself in such a deplorable place to get it, and why it was lamentable to see this young girl in the same place.

On the floor was a guy passed out against the far wall. From the way he sat, with his back propped up, Deana surmised this guy was on *old pro*; he probably made sure to pass out sitting up to help prevent choking on his own vomit. His head slouched against his shoulder, his open mouth exposed his rotten teeth. If not for the slightest of breathing motions, one might mistake him as deceased. With his disgusting hygiene and ragged clothing, his very presence was intrusive. He was another habitué that Deana ran into here and there, another broken person looking for the next thing to dull his senses. She never asked his name or his deal though. She never wanted to know. Establishing a connection with someone is intent to form a bond, become friends or partners, co-dependents or enablers. Deana had gone through that charade enough times to know better to tumble down that route. She put her trust in other drug-buddies before, believing their shared ideas and pleasures would hold them together, only to be burned and sometimes wind up in serious danger. In a few cases Deana was the danger: venturing further down the path to harder stuff, leaving her partner or whatever behind to pick up the shredded remanence of what used to be a kinship. It seemed to Deana that there was a twelve-month max for connections, before they turned away or she did.

Scrutinizing the miserable room coming more into focus, Deana noticed a few former friends were there actually, spread out around the room, mixed in with the debris. The couch was the only furniture one could buckled onto when the *dust* settled. They must have arrived and taken their dosage after she was already under, leaving them little other choice but swoon to the floor. Not that the inconvenience would, evidently, deter any real addict from taking a hit anyway. Each one of them, the friendship ended with Deana believing she was better off without them, and perhaps they were better off without her too. But here they all were, meeting again at the same low point, like a filthy class reunion. She wondered if they had the same reaction seeing her there too, or if they were too focused on getting their fix to even notice.

Amidst the collection of degenerates, Deana recognized a particularly regrettable face. Passed out against the wall directly across from her was the dirty trickster, Sean, an ex-lover who manipulated her into prostitution a few years earlier. Coming to terms that he would most likely never kick addiction before they met, Sean decided to embrace it, and devoted himself to obtaining more drugs – enough to keep, enough to sell. Deana had sought out Sean because she heard he was the only one, in the circle they both ran with, who might have iowaska. It turned out he did not, but the two hit it off instantly due to their shared preference for psychedelics at the time. Quickly into their toxic relationship, Sean turned

Deana onto crystal meth, which he chiefly employed to gain control over others. First, he ensured she became doped consistently enough to hardly notice or care she was being pimped out. Next, he began withholding her drugs until she complied willingly to his deals. Within six months Deana witnessed herself plummet to the cold tier of crack whore. One unusually sober morning she became cognizant of what was happening, and she summoned all her courage to run from Sean. Escaping while he was still asleep from the night before, certain she was heading for recovery from that point. That was her first time in rehab, and the last time she trusted anyone.

Sobriety did not last long though. Inevitably bumping into former acquaintances while attempting to get clean, it was too easy for her to fall for the sticky "Once more, for old time sake" line. Even after her relapse and continued abuse though, Deana consoled herself by repeating "at least you'll never be as bad as Sean." Repeating it, like a mantra in a misguided new age movement of drug therapy.

Now though, Deana found herself in the same place as Sean, their respective declining paths synchronized once again. The only elevated status she could claim was her place up on a couch opposed to his on the floor. She wanted to look away, but all she could see when turning her head was the young girl passed out beside her.

In a single position, Deana saw the person she swore to never become ahead of her and the person she started as to the side of her. Inspecting the room again, the other addicts there seemed like the transitional steps in between those two markers in her timeline. All their distorted faces were hers, sequentially over the years of narcotic use. Like some horrible house of mirrors, Deana felt trapped, kept from a normal existence and forced to roam in circles, perpetually having to confront her ill-conceived choices. Nowhere from this point could Deana turn that was an exit. The further she went down, there would be only more reflections. Even when Deana looked inward, she only saw them, and in seeing them she saw herself.

Suddenly, a tall, lanky man with no hair and irritated eyes discreetly entered the room, ending Deana's grim insightful moment. She was frightened at first, believing the man to be some phantom, possibly imagined. Soon though she recalled who he was exactly. This was Nathan, the dealer who lived here. Or maybe Nathan only did business here, and this was someone else's house. Deana could not remember now the full story clearly. Regardless, she revered Nathan to always be a welcoming and accommodating host. He typically was fully stocked with whatever drugs she was searching for and sold them at a fair price, at times at discount even for a returning customer. He was soft spoken and witty with a cockney accent, which the all the girls who came around giggled over. Even though he appeared obviously to shoulder the burden of his own drug problems, he was well composed and groomed and handsome.

    Nathan moved silently about the room observing all the wasted junkies, seemingly unaware Deana was awake and watching. He knelt over one of the men and did not hesitate to rummage through their pockets for whatever could be found inside. After pulling some loose cash from the addict's pants, Nathan moved on to the girl passed out next to him and proceeded to plunder her pockets with mechanical precision. And then, on to the next. Deana felt that invested trust in Nathan instantly disintegrate. She could recall walking out of that house, several times wondering where the few bucks in her purse had mysteriously vanished. And she could not stop herself from nervously questioning how many times he did something worse than loot her, or anyone really. It made sense now why he offered fair prices and discounts.

    Nathan abruptly stopped, like he sensed a disturbance it the air. His head snapped to face Deana, initially giving a scrunched up, grim expression. He looked like he did not recognize her. They stared at each other a short moment, and then Nathan relaxed. A familiar gentle smile came to his lips and a softness filled his eyes. The welcoming and accommodating host sprouting up to cover what was probably the grisly reality.

"Looks like some little-bitty precious woke up earlier than usual," he said quietly in that dense accent all the girls loved.

Deana gave no response, unsure if she was about to be punished for catching him or what. Standing up to tower over everyone again, Nathan reached into his pocket to pull out a small baggie with a hit of cosmic dust. Gracefully he approached the couch Deana was on and picked up her pipe, which had fallen beside her, between herself and the young girl's feet. Cleaning out the bowl of it with his dirty finger, with a small smirk he asked "How'd you like a blast-off on the house, astronaut? Something to keep space quiet again?"

Without waiting for Deana to answer, he stuffed the drug in the pipe knowing she would not turn down a free hit. Nathan extended his arm to offer her the pipe.

Deana felt her sight fall from him and become fixated on the refreshed instrument. Deep inside she knew it was a bad idea, that it would not undo what she witnessed a minute ago. At best there was a fifty-fifty chance of forgetting about it, or perhaps dismissing it as a drug dream. Even deeper inside though was the addiction calling out louder than reason. Cosmic dust was not cheap, and the withdrawal symptoms were said to be harrowing; she could not just quit right now. As she continued pitting her internal arguments, her arm unconsciously reached slowly for the pipe. Once her fingers were on its cool frame, the argument was over; her body had made the decision for the mind.

"There's a good girl now," Nathan said, stroking her dry hair softly, like comforting a confused infant. He stood there, watching to make sure Deana took the hit and did not go anywhere.

Deana, partly intimidated and partly eager, thought *"How could I refuse?"* as she lit up.

Yellow Roses

Another routine homicide in a city sustaining on recurrent crime. I arrive on the scene, and it's the typical patterns for a murder case: cheap motel room, corpse of some degenerate lying face down, shot to death, wallet's still there but cleared of all cash, various empty booze bottles, signs of a struggle, no revealing prints, and the window to the fire escape is open. The details are so commonplace I could arrest either the mistress or a disgruntled employee right now, with a fifty-fifty chance of having the actual murderer in custody. The mistress is even still here, she was the one who discovered the body. So, it wouldn't be out of my way to book her. Slap the cuffs on, mumble out those meaningless Miranda rights, fingerprints for consistency, lock the cell and call it an early one. Another bloody case closed one way or the other.

 Reasoning might suggest that by sticking around and giving a statement willingly, the mistress wasn't likely to be the killer. That a killer is inherently some dastardly caricature who flees immediately. I've been a detective in this sinkhole too long to fall victim to malarkey like that. It's not always the truth. But it doesn't matter, everybody's some color of criminal here. If I'm not locking them up for the right crime, I'm doing it for something they just haven't been caught for yet. That's how I see things at least. Copious amounts of murder cases will rattle your cage. You live in a perpetual state of compressed anger, distrust, and paranoia until you'd rather face a bullet than another day. At some point, you stop caring about even trying to prevent crimes. Especially murders. Let'em kill each other off. That's what they seem to want anyway.

    A fresh and brilliant spark pops through the muck of my sour brainwork however, as I survey the motel room: There are half a dozen yellow roses resting next to the body.

Not as if they were placed there deliberately, but like they were dropped carelessly. I kneel to observe the flowers more closely, and that spark pops again: Who buys yellow roses? Something's off about this case. I take the mistress aside for questioning. Her name is Bridgette Waters. Her name is too typical for me to find amusing. We run down the usual list, but the amount of shit I give wouldn't fill a soufflé cup about those details. She shares intimate information about her torrid affair with the dead man, who we ID as Jesse Solomon. The whole thing sounds painfully average. Solomon was married and used this motel as a meeting spot for things he wanted kept secret. Gambling, shady deals, and of course his girl on the side. Waters says he broke things off with her earlier that night. Coward didn't even do it to her face. He had a note sent attached to the roses, which were waiting for her that night when she came home from the diner where she works. The note had two words: "It's over". Assuming he'd be at the motel, placing a bet or hooking up with another woman, Bridgette marched over to chew him out and throw the flowers in his face. Solomon was dead when she arrived, and she ran downstairs to tell the desk clerk. I ask one of the drone officers hovering around the room to drive Ms. Waters home, but she says she prefers to walk. I really don't care how she gets home. As Waters leaves I ask why Solomon sent yellow roses, instead of the ordinary red. She shrugs subtly and quietly barked "Bastard probably thought they were cheaper or something".

I decide not to arrest the mistress. Not because she wouldn't suit as a sure conviction, but because I'm still considering that one unique aspect. Yellow roses represent joy, wellness. More relevantly, they mean friendship. More important, someone would've had to go out of their way to buy them. And despite what Bridgette Waters thinks, yellow are more expensive. Whenever a customer askes for roses, it's standard for florists to reach for the passionate kind. The kind that say Love, Romance. It's also a standard they buy a dozen. Half a handful of *'Let's just be friends'* don't tend to sit well with women, even if they are the other girl. No girl wants to be told they're not special enough. However, just seems too obvious for the mistress to have done it this time. She had the motive and was at the crime scene, sure, and maybe the situation is as clear-cut as it appears. Some small voice in me though refuses to believe my job has turned that depressingly uncomplicated. It's a voice I haven't heard in my head for a long time. This long dormant curious side of me has been revived by a minor change to one element in a mundane murder. It's absurd. Still, something's different here, and the person I used to be needs to know what.

    I stop by my office at the station to make an entry in my case journal before questioning the wife, recently turned widow. Covering the wall behind my desk are a variety of framed newspaper clippings, spouting headlines such as "Hero Detective Solves Murder Case" or "Local Detective Uncovers Underground Crime Ring". Trite that could replace "Hero Detective" with "Lucky Drunk" and "Murder Case" with "Humdrum Crime Blankety Blank". I take a moment and contemplate what these cases must have meant earlier on, for me to be proud enough to display the shorthand of them. That was a time when I was more easily surprised, and a Helluva lot more motivated. Unlike now, when I'm considering interrogating the vodka bottle in my desk in lieu of questioning the ex-Mrs. Solomon. There used to be a passion for my job. Ask questions, collect data, solve the mystery. It was an incomplete image, and I loved uncovering the link between the pieces. Over time each day turned into a puzzle that came already assembled, of a portrait I already have a variety of framed and mounted on the wall. For years, I silently begged for something novel and exciting to spring up. Until that bottom barrel optimism too became a static in the distance. Maybe I've become so desperate that the most minute detail can setoff sirens in my brain, like it's a damn five alarm forest fire. Half of me wants to forget it all and go home, the other half is aching to follow my gut that this is my redemption. In the end, this my job, and I'm going to do it if only for the paycheck. One swig from the vodka bottle, then I head off to the Solomon's residence.

At their home, Mrs. Solomon is so devastated when she hears the story, she takes exaggerated amounts of time alternating between uncontrollably sob and hyperventilate; She had no clue her husband had a defined double-life, and it took her a while to deal with that all. I take the opportunity, when more of her tears than words are coming out, to write down a grocery list on my notepad. Glancing around the parlor where we sit, I note an excessive collection of dolls and hand sewn quilts, and I surmise Mrs. Solomon is a bit of a shut-in. Could be the reason Jesse was screwing around, and why his wife was unaware. I should ask questions to be certain, to help color in the picture, but I just don't care that much. After a bit she settles down enough for us to finish the typical questions. Per usual, the widow is no help. Just about all the time it's because they're ignorant of what was going on. Sometimes though it's because they were the killer. Mrs. Solomon doesn't strike me that way though. In fact, she seems quite innocent. I get up to leave, but before I ask the only question I'm interested in. "Ma'am, did your husband buy you roses often?"

Instantly she makes a curious grimace, and asks forcibly what it has to do with anything. I reassure her it would be information pertinent to the case, but really it's to satisfy my own curiosity. Eventually I got out of her "No, my husband wasn't exactly a romantic type. I can't remember the last time he brought me flowers. And he was allergic to roses anyway. He couldn't even come near them. If he did buy me flowers, they'd be anything but roses."

My brain felt stimulated for the first time in years. Questions bubbled up like boiling water on a stove.

Who left roses for Bridgette Waters? Did someone stage manage her? Did they want her to come to that motel room, riled-up and looking for an argument, only to wind up standing above a lifeless body? Was that the reason for yellow roses, because their dispassionate significance might burn her enough she'd march unknowingly into a crime scene, putting herself in a compromising position? Was it the wife; had she found out about the affair, and set this whole thing up as frame? If so, was Mrs. Solomon the one who shot her own husband? Or was there no conspiracy? Was it all simply unrelated? Did Jesse Solomon have flowers sent to his mistress, with the intent to break it off? Maybe Solomon was murdered by someone else, perhaps over a gambling debt? Was it an argument gone wrong, or did it go exactly the way the killer wanted?

In all conceivable scenarios, I can't shake my intuition the yellow roses were the key to unlocking the truth. Either they would hold the connection, or ruling that out would present a more precise direction. Find out where they came from, discover who paid for them. That would be the start, and maybe everything falls in line afterwards. Maybe not.

Back at my office I make a list of every florist in town. There are five here scattered all over, but most had closed for the night. I tell myself I'm probably chasing mirages in a desert, and to hold off visiting the shops until the next day when they're all open. One of them opens at seven in the morning. Back at home, I watch myself set the alarm for five-thirty a.m. was a slight awe, and can't recall the last time I got up before the sun.

    Seven a.m. sharp, I'm waiting outside the first flower shop. The employee there is stunned to see a customer so early, he stalls for a moment before unlocking the door. I cut straight to it and ask if they sell yellow roses. They don't. As the day goes on, I discover yellow roses don't come easily. Visiting four out of the five florists, they reveal they've never sold yellow ones, and have never been asked about such oddities until today. The investigation is going as fast and fruitless as I should have expected. But, the owner of the fifth shop at least has a suggestion. An exotic flower shop, outside the city limits, might carry something other than red. A quick phone call confirmed they do, so I drive forty-five minutes to the location just to see for myself.

  Outside the limits of that ill-seeded metropolis, everything within sight seems much simpler and pure. Streets are cleaner, people are friendly enough. There is an air about that isn't polluted by the stench of cigarettes and alcohol, and an atmosphere not soiled by corruption. Someone like me wouldn't be needed here. Quite frankly, I feel like I'm devaluing the area just by driving down the road. This is where roses of all colors bloom.

Inside the targeted flower shop, the owner greets me warmly. I'm honest with him, telling him I'm investigating a homicide and need his cooperation. He's compliant and helpful and hands me his sales records upon request with no hostility or hesitation. According to their receipts they sold yellow roses at around eight o'clock at night, thirty minutes after Jesse Solomon died. The shop owner took the order himself. He tells me the flowers were sold over the phone using a credit card, and the customer paid a handsome price to have them delivered hastily into the city. They were delivered to address Ms. Waters gave me as her residence. The shop owner recalls it was a woman's voice that ordered the flowers. However, he claims there was no card insert request; the note "it's over" rings absolutely no bells. His delivery boy told him the recipient wasn't home when he came by, but he left the roses with the landlady. I get a copy of the receipt and credit card number, and thank the shop owner kindly for his help. Driving back, I can only concentrate on the case.

The coroner had estimated time of death at approximately seven-thirty p.m., roses purchased by phone at eight p.m., and Bridgette claimed she found Solomon dead just after ten. Game, set, and match. The mistress probably lied about being at work during the crime. Or was it made to look like that?

I check into the credit card number, but it comes back with an obvious fake name and fabricated information. Not a total surprise, just a disappointment. Phony credit cards are just another common thing here. It's a wonder how anyone makes any money at all, and a testament why more and more places are only accepting cash. We're all working on the dishonor system. Still, I feel like I'm getting somewhere. I know someone had to go out of their way to get yellow roses, so there had to be a significance. They were purchased after the murder, so it wasn't Jesse who sent them. The goodbye note was added later, and evidently said more than two little words.

I place a call to Bridgette Waters but she doesn't answer, so I head to her place for further questioning. At her apartment I pound on the door so loud her landlady comes out to scold me. She tells me Bridgette hadn't been home since furiously running out the night before, just before ten p.m. I immediately place a call to the widow, but there's no answer there either. I leave for the Solomon's residence, mashing up facts to juggle a picture of what the Hell was going on. At the Solomon's home there is no answer at the door. None of the neighbors have any idea where she might be, and no one can recall seeing her leave the house; they confirm my initial suspicions of she being a shut-in. Bridgette Waters said she worked at a diner downtown, so I stop by there. Speaking to a seasoned waitress, who claims she'd been there most of her life, I discover there is no Bridgette Waters on staff. With no picture to show her, I describe Waters best I can recall. The waitress says it sounds like Sarah Smith, but they have no picture either to confirm we are talking about the same girl. They don't even have any usable personal information for Smith. Only a terse employment application with her name, date of birth, city of residence, and a willingness to work minimum wage at all hours. The seasoned waitress tells me Smith left her shift a little early yesterday, just after eight p.m., feeling sick. If Smith is Waters, that would mean she left work after the murder happened. I thank the waitress and leave.

Feeling confused, I return to my office and record everything so far in my case journal. Every few hours I try getting ahold of the widow and the mistress without any luck. I keep going over what facts I know, but there are too many blank slots to form a viable theory. It seemed equally plausible either Bridgette or Mrs. Solomon ordered those damned roses, but was equally possible someone else did. It was equally implausible for either woman to have pulled the trigger, so it most likely was someone else did. Every time there was a *someone else* contingency added on to my thought. Someone else was a living shadow, capable of acting on its own without the aid of a flesh'n'blood counterpart. Or was the shadow only a smoke'n'mirrors trick? If it were someone else though, why have both girls vanished?

Two days passed, and the women go from murder suspects to routine missing persons. Different file, different case; a mystery to be solved before the mystery can be solved. I doubt they were bumped-off by someone else, their bodies would have been found. For the first time in years, a murder case in my files is left ongoing, open indefinitely. Whomever shot that man, they'll have put enough distance between them and the crime before I ever have the story figured out. No one in this loser community was going to exhaust themselves tracking suspects on the run, not plenty of other chumps around would suit as a conviction. I'd bet money one of those girls killed Jesse Solomon, and that they had put all their chips on the limp morals and apathetic lawmen of this city letting them crawl away. That same small part of me that wanted to believe this case couldn't be so obvious was the same part that wanted to admire them. Maybe thank them for shaking things up for a change. Although, that whole part of me would probably drown in a stream of alcohol, like many other parts before. This case would only be the last twinkling star in my ever expanding, ever darkening career.

A more ambitious detective might feel inspired and revitalized. But I'm just too old and too tied up in other routine murders to care.

Back at my office, on the wall behind my desk I post a handwritten headline that reads "Age Detective Lets One Slip Away". My way of reminding myself I'm finished, lest some case in the future fools me to believe otherwise.

The Turning Point

Dispirited already by the day's common letdowns, Cody felt his discontent sink even deeper when a knock came on the apartment door. The sound inserted a chill into the air, the type that usually accompanies unwelcomed news. This visitor threatened to interrupt the solitude Cody had become so accustomed that he preferred it now. He intended to ignore the disruption. While the knocking continued, he did not rise whatsoever from the sofa where he lay, uninterested in who might be responsible for the disturbance. None of his so-called friends ever dropped by unannounced, and considering his rent was paid up on time for once, Cody concluded the anonymous caller was most likely a solicitor. The building rarely saw them, but the ones that did manage to find their way in its halls always seemed to be lower riffraff than the tenants. Opening the door, or even shouting through it, would only give the solicitor motivation. He knew they would go away after a bit of time. For the time being, he decided to keep his face half-buried in the dirty couch cushion.

The knocking persisted longer than predicted, increasing in intensity and frequency. It nearly convinced Cody to get up and scream. But finally, it ceased, and Cody resumed his customary sulking in silence.

A new agitation started up however. This time from his cell phone vibrating on the coffee table. Cody sighed in defeat, understanding now the grueling universe was not accepting *no reply* for an answer today. He was not the smartest person, but he believed if the universe was pushing, there was no victory in pushing back. He reached for his phone and accepted the call. Keeping his eyes closed for a minimal sense of calmness, Cody put the phone to his ear but offered no greeting.

"Hello? ...Hello? Cody, you there?" asked a familiar voice on the line.

Cody hesitated a moment and then asked who was calling, curious why he knew that voice. Suddenly it reached him: It was the voice of his rarely seen cousin Peter.

"It's Peter. I'm outside you're place. You nearby?"

Although it was a pleasant surprise to hear Peter's voice, and a relief to find it was not a solicitor at the door, Cody was now embarrassed by his handling of the knocking situation. He did not want to let-on that he avoided answering the door usually, but he could not lie to a cousin he used to be so close with. "I'm here, I'm here. Just, give me a minute."

Cody hung up and pushed himself off the couch, groaning the whole way. He spent too much of his free time lying down, his body seemed to protest every time Cody moved off the couch or bed. He rolled his eyes over the pitiable condition of his tiny studio apartment. Straightening it up to look presentable would take more time than he wanted Peter to wait in the nasty hallway. Quickly brushing the crumbs off his shabby sweater and the unwashed hair out of his eyes, Cody prepped to appear bright and content while welcoming his cousin.

Peter meandered in and looked over the apartment with an expressionless face. Cody scrambled to collect and crumple the various fast food take-out bags littering the floor and coffee table, tossing them in an overflowing trash bin. He thought to move the half drank vodka bottle to a kitchenette cabinet, but figured none of the mess really could not be unseen by this time. Peter must have gleaned he was not in the best shape.

"Sorry for the mess," Cody apologized while he brushed off more stale crumbs from his sofa, "but I was just…away all weekend." It was a lie; one Cody knew was too transparent to stand. After it whizzed past his lips, he wondered why even bother trying to cover up the disaster his life had become. Surely his mother and Peter's still talked, glossing over their own shortcomings with gossip about the small achievements or shameful drubbings of their children.

Peter was offered a seat with a gesture from Cody, but he declined with a mute wave. Cody did blame him for wanting to stay clear of the feculent furniture. Dressed in nice grey slacks, a crisp white button-down shirt and black tie, but with his wonted bomber style jacket, Peter looked like he was making an effort for someone important. Whatever his cousin did with himself in the five years since they saw each other last, it certainly included more maturity and respectability than Cody gained.

Averting his eyes, Cody desperately wanted to avoid what he thought was coming: Peter's brutal commentary over the unfolded laundry scattered on the floor and furniture, the odor of spoiled food coming from the trash can, and vacant alcohol bottles claiming residence around his bed. Peter was seldom judgmental, but when he did speak up it felt like standing in a wind tunnel. The insults and contempt came with such extraordinary force one was nearly blown down. Not a full minute passed since Cody let Peter into his home, and already he wished he had ignored the phone buzzing. It would have prevented this disarmingly humiliating position. Every second Peter kept quiet, Cody felt like he grew smaller, imagining he might poof away like magic, at last spared from the shame of how wrecked his life had become.

"You never could clean up right," was all Peter eased out finally. "Doesn't matter, I'm not here for that."

Cody sat on the armrest of the sofa, placing his feet on the cushion to look relaxed. Relieved Peter withheld his criticisms mostly, Cody instinctively shifted into a humorous manner. His cousin and he used to routinely engage in a sort of comical joust, and Cody thought this might be their chance to resume. "Why not? You look hot in the French maid outfit."

Peter did not reflect a playful attitude back. Instead he stood with his hands in his pockets and a solemn face of stone, unable to even break into a smirk. His sternness put Cody more ill-at-ease. Though the two cousins did not see each other as much as they used to, their reunions always were spiced with Peter's wisecracking. Peter picked on Cody like a bully, and Cody returned the digs right back, both understanding it was a sign of affection. This visit now however was building up to be austerely blunt, with Peter not bearing jokes. So, Cody peddled back into a more serious demeanor. He felt a sudden need to get whatever this was out in the open and over. "So then, to what do I owe this unexpected pleasure?"

"Have you heard from Frank?" asked Peter stiffly.

Cody briskly slid off the couch and stepped towards the tiny kitchenette window, which overlooked a warped community basketball court. He had no immediate response to that question. At least not one that could be put into favorable words. Frank was a name he wanted to never hear again, and a man he wished to entirely forget. He tried to maintain a silly-sophisticated tone to mask his anger.

"To which Frank to do speak of? Frank, my brother who stole all my savings? Frank, my brother who slept with my fiancé? Frank, my brother who forged my name on some pharmacy scripts? Frank, my brother who ruined my credit, leading me to dwell in rat holes like *this* palace?" Cody faced back around to Peter and leaned against the window "I mean, you gotta admit I know so many Franks."

Cody could see Peter was not finding any humor in his reply. But, he knew of no reason to be serious where his brother Frank was concerned. Frank was the older brother, the one who should have paved the way and watched out for his younger sibling. On the contrary, he acted like a kid brother his whole life, and somehow got away with everything like a kid brother too. Frank repeatedly had to be bailed out or picked up, was frequently stuck in a bad state of affairs from which he could not, or would not, dig himself out. And every time, he left someone else, usually Cody, behind to pick up the pieces. When they were kids, it was fights with neighbors Frank started but Cody would have to finish; Meaning Cody got beaten up plenty. When they were teens, it was drinking binges gone dangerous, which Cody pulled Frank out of. When they were young adults, things became worse.

When Frank was twenty-two and Cody was twenty, Frank asked for three hundred dollars to pay off a gambling debt. Cody was too sick with a flu to go to the bank, so gave his debit card to Frank to get the cash. Frank never came back. He drained Cody's account, which included a five-thousand-dollar inheritance from their then recently deceased grandmother. Two years passed before Frank resurfaced, apologizing and promising to return the stolen money in small increments. He did not stick around to make good on any of his words though. Returning home to find his little brother engaged, Frank took Cody and his fiancé Lilly out to celebrate. Cody could not recall most of the evening. But he certainly remembered waking up on the couch, while his brother and Lilly lie naked on Cody's bed together. Frank just denied everything and ran off again, leaving Lilly to take all the blame. The wedding was cancelled, Cody began to drink heavily, and Lilly disappeared like a broken dream. Frank returned three years later, this time a sickly alcoholic. He looked so pathetic then that when he requested only to be taken to a doctor and examined, Cody could not refuse. He figured if he could be the bigger brother once again, Frank had to start making things right. Instead, Frank vanished from the doctor's office, never meeting Cody back in the waiting area.

Cody found out Frank walked off with the doctor's prescription pad, and eventually was arrested for questioning. Frank was using Cody's name on the scripts for some unknown reason, and the police suspected the two brothers could be in cahoots. Of course, Cody was cleared of the charges. The whole experience however soiled his perception of life, turning him naturally bitter and cynical towards everyone. That somber and sarcastic attitude he developed cost him jobs and relationships, pulling him further away from a normal life. When trying to reassemble his life, Cody found it almost impossible. Once again due to his brother. Frank had started habitually opening credit lines under Cody's name and social security number. Cody's credit was destroyed before he was thirty, and he was forced to live and work wherever background checks were neglected. At thirty-two now, Cody felt a complete absence of self-respect. He trusted no one, and consistently felt like he was merely waiting for his life to expire.

Excluding himself, Cody wondered how many others out there his brother used up dry. Which was the most painful wound: He felt his brother viewed him no differently than a naive stranger. That made him feel like the biggest fool in a line of suckers.

With all that pent-up frustration charging an irritated grimace on his face, Cody waited for Peter to explain why, after all these years, he would pop by only to chat about an undesired topic like Frank.

"I mean your brother Frank, who's dying of cancer," Peter laid down coldly.

Cody turned away again, ashamed of himself. Not that he could have known what message Peter was there to deliver, but ashamed for having let Frank become the butt of his jokes. Even after all the rotten tricks Frank unfairly thrusted upon him, a death sentence was not the justice Cody wanted for his brother. On the contrary, Cody desperately subconsciously hoped Frank would turn a new leaf one day, and finally become an older brother prepared to make things right in the family. Though Cody never said it out loud to anyone, not even his mother, he daydreamed of Frank randomly showing up at his door with the earnest intentions to redeem himself. What was received though was his cousin arriving to play surrogate for a Frank presumably too sick to come himself. Cody wondered if Peter was even there on Frank's request, or if he was there to attempt some sort of forced reunion without Frank's knowledge. In any event, Cody felt he would most likely be doing the reconciling.

    Standard questions Cody thought people might ask in this situation shot around his mind, but a petty side of him was holding back for want to appear unaffected by the news. Besides, Cody had been burned too many times by

Frank, and he could not help being a touch suspicious this was another scam to elicit sympathy. And through sympathy Frank typically sought money for gambling or drugs. Still, a better side of him genuinely needed to know all the information before condemning. Cody felt at war with himself, concerned for the wellbeing of his family as much as self-preservation from them. Uncertain which side of himself was stronger, Cody simply did not say anything to advance the conversation. What he wanted was to look away long enough for Peter to take a hint and leave. If Peter exited as quickly as he came, without another word spoken, Cody believed he might convince himself it did not matter what happened to Frank; there was half a vodka bottle in the cabinet, to dilute the memory of hearing his brother's health was dire enough to be labeled "dying."

Drinking had become Cody's customary method of dealing with the stress Frank yielded. Then eventually alcohol was essential for just getting through every day. A scared side of him wanted things to stay that way. Life had changed enough for Cody in his short time, and for more changes to be on the horizon was demotivating. Alcohol afforded him a crutch with which to limp through life numbly. Any prospect of coming out of his sort of waking coma felt exhausting. Ironically, life seemed safer estranged and alone from the world than connected to it.

Cody stared out the window above the sink in the kitchenette, simply unable to reply appropriately.

"Listen…" Peter started up with a soft voice, "I know how Frank is, and I've been screwed by him too. Too many times. But face it, he's family.

"Family is just a word, remember?" Cody cut in, continuing to look out the window. "We decided that a long time ago, the three of us. The night grandpa was buried, and the whole family fought over the junk in his house. Remember that? Even Frank was one of the reasonable ones that time." Cody massaged his face, trying to conjure clear memories of that night. "I was…eleven, I guess, so Frank was thirteen. You were fifteen. The three of us sat in the shed, because there was nothing in there but garden tools that nobody wanted. We couldn't believe how greedy all his kids got, yelling about who got the crappy knick-knacks. You snuck a beer out, because you knew no one would be watching. You and Frank tried to split the can but couldn't stand that taste. You wouldn't even let me try it, you just threw it out in the yard somewhere." Cody paused, sensing Peter smirk, finally, behind him.

That night the three of them became as closed as they would ever be. They talked in that shed all night. The bonding was one of the most important moments in all their lives, even though Cody could not recall now what they talked about. The content was not what mattered,

Cody knew that, but the moment did. They felt more adult than anyone in the family at that time.

Cody shook off the warm feeling that memory brought. "Anyway, we knew then that family wasn't what we were told, or what we assumed. Family wasn't just something you're born into. Family is the people you trust, blood has nothing to do with it. In fact," Cody tapped on the kitchenette counter with a little laugh, driving home is point, "I think those were Frank's words. Blood has nothing to do with it. Turned out to be true. Blood had nothing to do with it."

"Precisely, Frank's words. He meant them and still does," Peter jumped back in, hinting that he already spoke to Frank. "He still trusts you, which makes you family in his book. How is that for convenient-logic?"

'Convenient-Logic' was a term Cody and Frank coined when they were teenagers, meant to mock their aunts and uncles' tendency to choose sides based on which was most beneficial to themselves at that moment. Cody recalled a time when he never would have expected his brother to turn out so much like them. Although he was a troublemaker from a young age, Cody did not foresee Frank becoming such a disgrace, nor guess their bond could become helplessly fractured. Now Convenient-Logic appeared to swing around and sucker-punch Cody; Frank was in a dire spot once again, and he looked towards Cody and Peter for support.

Cody held his gaze out the window. Three young boys had started playing hockey across the street on the world-worn basketball court. Some bad call must have happened, because the boys started to argue all of the sudden. The kids appeared to yell at each other for a few seconds, and then resumed their game like nothing had happened. It reminded him of how close he, Frank and Peter were once. Playing, then a fight, followed immediately by mended fences and the resumed game.

There seemed to be nowhere Cody could look to escape the reminder. One way or another, the situation at hand demanded immediate attention, a long overdue mended fence. It had to be addressed and dealt with, or else the game would never resume. Then again, Cody thought, there was an end to all games, and every game has a winner and a loser. It was difficult for Cody to identify which one he was in the end.

"Listen..." Peter started up again with the softer voice, "I'm not saying forget about everything Frank's done. He hasn't forgotten it. I'm just saying maybe it's best the two of you work things out while there's time." Peter turned around towards the door, having said what he had come to and now knowing when to leave. "I'm heading to his place now. Aunt Madeline had his address for a while. Turns out he's been living just across the state line all this time." Peter opened the door, adding "Maybe I'll stop on the way at that hotdog joint we used to hang at...give you a chance to catch up." And just before Peter closed the door he said "Ketchup. Get it?"

There was the funny side of Peter slipping out, even if it had evidently gotten stale. Cody felt like he was hearing his cousin again.

Without an official goodbye Peter left, closing the door behind him gently. Cody remembered how loud Peter used to slam doors even when he was trying to be quiet. In fact, he was always loud. One could hear him come, with the loud, clunky boots he used to wear. Cody just then realized Peter had not been wearing boots today. Peter also used to never wear anything under that bomber jacket except black t-shirts and blue jeans, without care when the occasion demanded a more formal effort. Frank and he used to joke about marketing that combination as an all-purpose garb called "the Peter" to department stores. He wore that jacket with some jeans to his own father's funeral. Cody had always viewed that look as an example of how some things never change.

    Irrefutably though, Peter was just standing there in the room a minute prior, wearing the same style jacket but with different clothes underneath. That image stuck around in his head, impressing a hopeful notion upon his mind.

Cody mused that if even at the smallest degree people have the capacity to change, then maybe that is enough room for larger changes: Changes of mind, and changes of heart. Change was an immutable element to life.

    Regardless of what Cody did, the days would never look the same. They would always look like mournful sunset, counting down the hours until there was no turning back. So much had happened in the past few minutes, and it all made Cody feel suspended above a disposition that he had regrettably grown comfortable in; the somber security of belief that it was better to be alone than be connected to someone that might fail you.

A faint sense of compassion vibrated inside him, shaking loose the numbness that laid like dirt upon his conscious. Cody wanted to not be estranged from his brother anymore, and an opportunity was open if he only took the leap. There was not a measure of guarantee Frank had finally turned that new leaf, even in the face of cancer. But Cody felt that assuming the worst was accepting defeat, and accepting defeat was denying a chance for change in the right direction. The universe was pushing, and there was no victory in pushing back.

Understanding he could be making the wrong move, Cody grabbed his jacket and headed out to catch Peter at that hotdog joint.

BPM Counter

At what felt like two hundred beats per minute, a hangover related headache was already up and active when Ariel's eyes squinted open. Poor decisions from the previous night to stay out and keep partying after her set were to blame. The first coherent thought in her bleary mind was the same one she had every morning: *"I've got to pull it back a bit."* This chorus of regret-spawned determination repeated in her head again and again, offbeat to the headache. Ariel could tell by the slivers of sunbeams breaking through the special light-blocking curtains it was too late in the day to remain defeated in bed for much longer. Regardless of how distorted she felt, it was time to get up.

    Ariel pushed herself off the bed and meandered to the bathroom, keeping steady with her hand on the wall for support. Catching a look at herself in the bathroom mirror, she hunched over the sink with her arms braced on either side of it. The morning dizziness would subside, it always did, but the morning appearance was harder to deal with. The dried out condition of her skin, the sagging under her burned out red eyes, her hair stale from too much product, and smudged lipstick and eyeliner. It all was a stark reversal of how she looked only hours earlier, before coming home from the club and passing out on the bed. *"Maybe I just need to cut out the alcohol. It can't be the weed, it's got to be the alcohol,"* Ariel thought, glossing over her casual use of ecstasy only because she didn't take any the night before. She never rolled during a gig, or at least not before her set. Of course, she knew refraining from drinking at the clubs was not going to happen. It was too easy to follow along when everyone else was smashed there. Also, she could sense people for some reason did not trust a DJ that did not drink and roll. It was hard enough for a woman to get recognition as a DJ to begin with, let alone a sober one.

Without bothering to check her phone for messages or updates, Ariel stepped into the tub. The revivifying feeling of a hot shower was needed more than missed drunk text messages and social media praise. She appreciated all the attention, but not at that time of day. The shower was a safe zone for Ariel. She trained herself to leave all concerns on the other side of the curtain, making the inside a space to wash her mind clean. With her head rested against the tile wall, eyes closed, she surrendered to a high-flow water streams colliding with her forehead and racing down her body. Steam from the temperature felt cleansing to her pores. Ariel stood immobile in that space until she was fully awake and coherent.

After leaving the comfort of her bathroom, she checked the time and saw it was one o'clock in the afternoon. Day had become her nights, afternoon her mornings, and she wondered if the transposition was healthy. A knotting in Ariel's belly screamed that it was not natural, for her anyway. She sat on her bed to take in a minute more of relaxation before starting her day.

The blinking light on her phone signaled that life had started without her. She checked the notifications while in her bath robe: 4 voicemails from the old-fashioned friends, 22 text messages from the more modern ones, 37 Facebook comments on DJ Ariddle's page – Ariel's stage name - and 5 updates on her personal profile, 40 Twitter notifications, 5 emails in her personal box and 35 in her professional. Plus 2 failed alarms.

'Damn, I must be doing something right,' Ariel thought in response to the increased social media notices, which rose gig after gig.

Ariel dropped the phone on the bed and picked out something modest to wear for her routine coffee shop visit, where she would answer all cosmetic fan comments before addressing anything business related. Dressed in blue jeans, flip flops, an old t-shirt and a baseball cap, Ariel was a broad contradiction to her performing image. She would be practically unrecognizable to any clubber as she walked to the coffee shop. Once there, Ariel ordered a strong espresso and found a cozy spot to plod through and acknowledge the fan tweets and comments. Per usual, amongst the humdrum remarks about how her set "rocked" – even though she was a trance DJ who specifically excluded any rock'n'roll influences from her mixes – there were the virtual catcalls from jacked-up douche bags, who thought posting smutty comments on her social pages, or more pathetically by forwarding dick pics, was a clever idea. Ariel deleted and blocked those users instantly, fretting over the fact they were becoming as frequent as any other fan. She worried about what actions someone might take if they saw her out, going about her personal routine. She certainly did not make enough money to hire a body guard, and security at the gigs frequently focused more on peddling drugs off to the side than attending to their actual positions. Vulgar jerks and obscenities on the page were simply part of the picture, Ariel was told once by a club owner. As much as she hated to admit it, that seemed to be true. Still, there were always the more innocent, appropriate comments, which she could not deny boosted her ego and validated her struggle in the music and nightclub world.

    Making headway in the music scene is hard for everyone. If anything it was substantially easier for DJs to earn money and notoriety than other acts. The crowds who went to those places and attended those shows typically had extra cash to dish out. With the mix of alcohol and ecstasy usually melting coherence away, their money dropped as quick as their sweat. That generally made club owners more generous when paying the talent. Plus, a DJ needs less equipment, stuff that did not require tuning or restringing, which in the long run made it cheaper to play. A 2 turntable mixdeck, headphones, and a laptop with some basic software. That was it. Most of which could be purchased second hand for starter DJs. After gaining some experience, moving up in the scene and earning better pay, one could incorporate better mixers and upgrade their equipment. But until then one could get by with the basics. A lot of the clubs Ariel played provided the AP system too. Patrons routinely came to dance and get laid. So long as the music kept pushing towards that offramp, there was applause.

The simplicity of the genre did not mean it was a cakewalk though. Gathering the right equipment and learning all the trade tricks took Ariel quite a while to tackle, consuming the majority of her free time and disposable income. When she was starting out, the applause and morning after digital thumbs-up felt like all she needed to justify the late nights and near empty bank account. Naturally that sentiment did not last forever, not when it was costing more to play the shows than what she was getting back at the time. Physically and financially it was exhausting her to play shows then. And of course, there was the consistent uphill battle of being a woman in the DJ business. Club owners loved hiring women DJs because of sex appeal, but did not give a damn about their skills. Not only did Ariel feel her talents were going unnoticed, which was needed to pass on word of mouth to other clubs for more shows and exposure, she worried that at any time she might be bumped or passed over for a hotter girl DJ. Audiences responded likewise for the same reasons, so long as the ratio of boys to girls on the floor favored the former. Which it almost always did. Even under the superficial layer of all that, no one naturally trusted a women DJ for some elusive reason.

Ariel could recall a night out at a club: She was not spinning that night, just taking in the scene for inspiration. Some boy there, supposedly dragged to the place by a friend trying to score drugs, "enlightened" her with the words "women who spin are just trying to play with the big boys. It's like a kid sister trying to keep up with older brother." Ariel detested gender biased assumptions and wanted to reply "If you think women spin tunes to compensate for not having a penis, maybe it's because yours doesn't quite cut it" in protest to reflect his infantile manner. She held back from saying anything though, lest she be labeled a "Bitch" for speaking her mind. Insults spread like wildfire, and she could see getting turned down for future gigs because some club owner heard she was *bitchy* to customers or hard to deal with in general. Instead she walked away from him, hoping her silence said enough. Although she knew it wouldn't, not with a small minded boy. The encounter had ruined the evening, and discouraged her from pursuing music for a short while. It was not the first time she had to deal with some comment like that, and sadly was not the last time she had to walk away instead of fighting back.

Although excited earlier on, in the beginning, Ariel was finding less and less refreshment reading fan comments overall. It was just another part of the job.

Ariel left the coffee shop and settled back at her apartment in front of her laptop. Reading all the business related emails and newsletters first, she responded to any gig offers to work out her event schedule. More places were starting to offer slots, and almost every place she spun requested her back sometime after. The notion that these places were always only after getting her pretty face on a flier to promote their club loomed over Ariel. But, she was nowhere near famous or rich enough to turn down too many offers. If it paid well and did not conflict with another gig, she took whatever. A lot of the clubs were more dingy looking when the house lights were on and felt very unsafe. She hated playing those gigs, but she needed the money and notoriety to hopefully get out of them for good.

After going through all work emails, Ariel checked any replies to her applications as a freelance designer. Finding there were only a few rejections and no approvals, Ariel slouched back and studied the empty spot on the wall where her degree in graphic design used to hang. Initially she put it there as a reminder that with hard work she could achieve her goals. That hokey, self-fueled inspiration dampened after eighteen months of rejections, and anchored the next year as more rolled in. That degree remained unused while she had no choice but to work idle shifts at pointless, frustrating jobs. Until one day when that piece of paper felt like a mockery instead of inspiring, and she was compelled to pull it down. It was during that time her then-boyfriend gifted her a used mixdeck to cheer her up; he thought it might serve as a hobby as she became fond of trance music recently before. The interest grew from hobby to skill, and she found herself spinning initially at friends' parties. Then acquaintances' parties. And finally, less than a year later from starting, she got her first gig, at some very shady place near the low end of town. Another year had gone by since that, and DJing had become something Ariel just did now. A part-time job was still necessary to supplement income, but nothing as bad as she worked prior. The confidence from performing evidently leaked into her latent desire to work in graphic design, and she recently started applying for freelance work. Of course, not having much work history as support, she was still getting nowhere in that field. Ariel closed her laptop, wanting to not think about it anymore. She had a set later that night, a weekend gig, and wanted her head clear.

She made a small lunch and watched an episode of some mindless TV show. Afterwards she tried meditating. Which was a new attempted undertaking for Ariel, one she was not sure she was actually getting the hang of. She certainly did not have the funds to drop money on a legitimate instructor. In fact, their course fees were considerably ridiculous. Reading a few online instructional sites and watching a couple videos was enough to get started, she thought. Ultimately, meditation was too silent,

Ariel was starting to find. After a few failed passes, she gave up and grabbed her mp3 player, put on a new mix one of her friends made and took a long walk. That was more revitalizing than meditation. On the walk she popped into a cheap retailer, where treated herself to some new clothes for the show later. Subsequently she purchased a few albums at a used record store she frequented. The owner there helped promote her work and had even gotten her a few gigs. He talked to Ariel more like a person than a commodity, and that was a huge reason why she returned often. She felt relaxed and comfortable there, and not like she was putting on act for work. Spending close to an hour shopping around, Ariel checked out with some classic country compilations. Old country music was a bit of a guilty pleasure, stretching back to her childhood and grandfather. Subconsciously, she also liked the notion of buying something most people did not expect her to, while feeling a little proud of not being restricted to only a few avenues of music. After that she returned home to browse around the internet for a while, checking local news and updated blogs. Following a quick microwaveable dinner, she then prepared for the night.

    She pulled cash from the personal safe hidden under her bed, to use for cab rides to and from the club. Cabs felt safer than taking the train, especially during those tiny hours between late night and early morning when Ariel was usually heading home. It always felt like a time where few decent people were out, and intoxicated women were easy prey for the fiends that were. There was some apprehension growing lately though about getting into what was essentially a stranger's car. Getting a vehicle of her own was not possible though, not with the payments, insurance, maintenance and, unavoidably, tickets and parking. Cabs were the best option; she just kept a hand close to her mace until safely home again. Ariel put the money in her gig-bag so as not to forget it, and then went about the rest of her routine.

    In the bathroom mirror she applied her make-up, intentionally balancing the façade of cosmetics to highlight her features but also stay reserved. Hair flat ironed, dyed black with just a few ocean blue extensions. The same delicate care was extended when selecting an outfit from the bedroom closet. A somewhat low cut, dark sleeveless shirt, but with a brightly colored moto jacket over it. As always, black denim pants, capped with some sort of boot. Never a dress, or even a skirt. Ariel wanted to look the part of a club DJ, but she had to draw a line. Regrettably, the regulation was for the aim to prevent boys from viewing her as someone "asking for it". She could not risk attracting the wrong attention, any more than naturally sprouted simply from being a woman in the DJ booth. These details of the business sometimes made Ariel feel like a prisoner, allowed to see the sky but confined in her ability to follow it to the horizon to which it settled.

Ariel took a look in the mirror at DJ Ariddle, a confident alternate side of herself that surfaced only during gigs. In this form, Ariel started to feel empowered to take on the night, both the work and the potential annoyance from the crowd. DJ Ariddle handled the all-around pressures that Ariel ever could. Satisfied with her image for the evening, DJ Ariddle grabbed her bag and headed out.

Her destination was Trypnotic, a dance club focusing on trance and acid jazz. Sergio the owner let her in through the alley entrance when she arrived. He was a nice enough guy, never treating her like a piece a meat –

although she had heard some rumors about him copping a condescending attitude behind closed doors with other women. He always paid decently however and in cash, right at the end of the night. Some owners or managers tried to stiff DJ Ariddle, by claiming they would transfer her cut to her account or pay her double next time. Neither of which would actually happen. She learned overtime to write "payment due the night of the gig" in her emails back to clubs who asked her to spin. If one did not specify, they might get underpaid or not at all. Chuck, a bouncer at Trypnotic and Ariel had a drink after she had set up her gear, as they waited for other employees to arrive. Most places required her to be there a few hours early, before the club opened, despite the fact it never took long to set up and run a sound check. Shortly before the doors opened for business, Sergio turned on the stereo and Ariel retreated to the employee lounge. Not all clubs permitted her access to be in the employees only areas, leaving her to mix with the crowd, which more often than not proved troublesome. Every patron either wanted to chat with her endlessly, push their own mixes hoping to get connected, or offer her drugs and take her back to their place. DJ Ariddle was reaching a point where the only reason she wanted to come to any club was to play; Ariel was developing a distaste for common clubers. She valued the benefit of waiting anywhere away from them. She wondered if she could start writing that into her email contracts as a sort of rider.

Trypnotic began to fill up quickly, with some customers specifically there to see DJ Ariddle's set. That was what Sergio was telling her at least. She passed the time in the back listening to music on her MP3 player, trying to retain that calm and confidence she plucked earlier in the night, back in her own apartment. From time to time this happened, when the initial flush of ease from transforming into DJ Ariddle rescinded just enough for Ariel to question things. She silently asked if this scene was really what she wanted to be a part of, and was it worth the pressures and harassments and late nights and the broken relationships, and on and on. If these questions came earlier in the nights though, Ariel might never leave her apartment again.

DJ Ariddle looked at the clock and saw there was five minutes until her set. Those last five minutes were always exasperating. Ariel had come to call it the *Quake Time*. Everything inside and around her would feel like it was quivering so much that she might become sick. The feeling reminded her of the one earthquake she witnessed, when she was thirteen on vacation with her dad. The event lasted only seconds, but the knowledge that the ground on which she stood could tremor like that at any time, that terrified Ariel to that point she vomited on her dad's shoes. Quake Time was heavy with the same sort of uncertainty of what could and could not be relied upon. Almost every time it was accompanied by an urge to walk away from the DJ act then and there. Rejection was not what she feared, her sets always elicited loud applause and praise. It was the paranoid side-effects of the proliferating favor DJ Ariddle was accumulating. Week to week it seemed DJ Ariddle was attracting larger pools of fans, which meant more people in the club tried to get closer to her, party with her, drink with her, sleep with her, whatever. More and more she felt she was losing ways to circumvent the probable and improbable hazards of the night, and during the last five minutes before set there seemed to be no chance of running from them.

During this overcome moment, Sergio came around to ask if she was ready to start. Whether she was or not, Ariel forced herself to say *YES*. She hesitated a moment, and then followed him out. DJ Ariddle took the stage, and there was applause as the lights dimmed out and the house music quieted; her intro music faded in.

Before she could catch herself, DJ Ariddle was spinning and mixing beats and riffs. It was as if someone else took Ariel over, and she watched them wield a craft they had mastered across a lifetime. She crossfaded into her own world: the beats, the synths, the samples, the consistent pace, the jubilant vibe, the neon lights, they all came together, forming a singular high note. The crowd evaporated like faceless souls from a dream, and DJ Ariddle was the sole presence on her own plateau of electronic existence, breathing in music and living like light. She felt here and gone instantaneously. That state of mind meditators always raved about, but Ariel could never reach. Everything went in slow motion, so she could take as much time as she liked to savor each note. Each fragment of time was alive and still, a living picture content in its space.

And yet, it was suddenly over.

That plane of emotional ecstasy seemed to last forever, but when DJ Ariddle caught the timer on her laptop read she was nearly sixty minutes in, the transcendence completely faded out. She knew she had to bring the set to a close, bow off, and let the staff push their crowd for more booze sales.

After the music stopped and the set was over, DJ Ariddle was so amped up that she did not realize she was heading off the stage directly to the main floor; DJ Ariddle wanted to meet her fans, as Ariel wanted to avoid them. By the time Ariel's initial concerns resurfaced fully from their momentary slumber, Ariel was closer to the bar than the stage and employee area, and the intensifying apprehension called for a drink to soothe her trembling hands. Along the way she was greeted by so many strangers, who wanted to chat with her forever, push their own mixes, and offer her drugs and take her back to their place. It was like walking down the escalator from Heaven to Hell. Ariel tried to keep a smile, be cordial and maybe even accommodating while she approached the bar. At least people stepped aside to let her in, as if she were royalty or something.

Ariel asked for a vodka soda, and indulged those around who complimented her set, her looks, her whatever. She gulped her drink down to escape the banality of some chauvinist ass nearby making overtly sexual comments towards her, and immediately asked for another from the bartender as the guy persisted with disregard for her ignorance towards him.

The ambient chatter increased, deafening any chance of sensible interaction. The pattern was coming full circle, and she could see another regretful morning rotating in.

Phantom Creatures in the Woods

Frightened awake by a loud, inhuman noise, Ellen hardly had the sense to keep quiet and still in her tent. She rustled around groggily for the flashlight, which was supposed to beside her inside the sleeping bag. Through a hazy waking state though, she vaguely remembered tossing it somewhere after repeatedly rolling onto the hard casing while trying to fall asleep.

Before the flashlight could be found, Ellen realized how nearby the disruptive noise had sounded. Whatever made it might be just outside the tent and might be attracted to a sudden burst of light coming from within. Ellen waited motionless for a moment, trying to breathe calmly and gently. Nothing broke the silence, suggesting it was safe to move a little. She brushed slowly over the thin bottom layer of the tent with her hands. The ground was cold and uneven, and more uncomfortable now than when laying down at bedtime. At last her hand touched the handle of the flashlight. Clutching it close to her chest,

Ellen resumed waiting stationary, apart from some nervous shaking.

The noise, what now seemed like a mournful wailing, came again. It was too low pitched to be a wolf, and too smooth to be a bear. In fact, Ellen could not readily match it with any animal she ever heard. It came again, only this time from farther off. With a certain perceived buffer between it and she, Ellen felt brave enough to open the flap of the tent and peer out.

Icy winter air assailed her face, pushing to the limits of discomfort. She had been so startled upon first waking that the cold weather was of no concern. Now though, the climate was impossible to ignore. With an increasing mix of unpleasant conditions, Ellen gleaned a new understanding why most people did not to go camping during winter or by themselves. She regretted the impulsive decision to do both this weekend. About the only factor in her favor at this point was no snow had fallen. The car ride to the area had taken longer than mapped, the hike up to the campgrounds had been more precarious than suggested, and the air felt approximately fifteen degrees colder than forecasted. But the predicted snow never happened. This was only the first night, and Ellen was questioning if she should have come at all; deciding in this moment now to leave first thing in the morning. She was notorious for making snap decisions that relied heavily on gut feelings over forethought.

Nevertheless, here she was now, and with a swelling sense of dread she definitely did not anticipated.

    Again the wailing came, even more distant this time. It was moving away from the campgrounds, farther into the surrounding woods. More awake and consciousness now, Ellen thought the noise sounded comparable to a wounded cry for help; from something in pain, solo in the vast darkness. Ellen found herself wondrously sympathetic to whatever was out there. Against better judgment, she shined a beam from her flashlight onto the tree line. Nothing unexpected was out there, and the area appeared safe. Receding back into the tent, Ellen gathered her boots and coat with the intention to investigate outside. Her impetuous nature in full effect.

Echoes of her mother's protests on camping alone whirled around Ellen's mind. As did the hypothetical disapprovals her friends might express now, if any of them knew she was there. She had left in such a flash Thursday evening, there was no consideration to tell anyone else she was going by herself. What beratement they would lather upon her, for preparing to venture into the darkened wilderness after an unidentified creature. Swiftly Ellen dismissed all the mental chatter of what others might say. Blather only discouraged real adventure. Part of the reason Ellen liked to go camping was a thirst for adventure, a chance to experience something beyond the banality of everyday life. No one she knew was ever willing to, or even remotely interested in leaping into a situation which was not entirely drawn out for them. They were comfortably trapped in a routine. When she camped with friends in the past – the ones that would go camping - inspiring any of them to even hike off trail was a laborious debate. At this moment though, with her hiking boots tied and jacket zipped, and nobody physically there to veto the motion, there was no shrinking back. A phantom creature was roaming nearby, paging Ellen to answer the call of curiosity and thrill.

She took half a minute to calm herself. Although the wilderness promised anything other than to be boring, Ellen understood ample room was open for potential danger. That possibility was not enough to make her reconsider, it only meant Ellen was mentally preparing herself for things to turn out regrettable. Her approach to life had always been *'act now, regret it later.'* That tenacious motto had also nearly led to a breakup with her fiancé Sean only a day prior. She and Sean were supposed to be there together this weekend, on a short getaway to simmer down from the stress that goes along with planning a wedding. But, a petty argument over floral arrangements matured into a fight the night before they were scheduled to leave.

They had ordered bouquets of white and purple flowers for her bridesmaids. When the bouquets came in though, they were blue and purple. The florist claimed she could correct the mistake by the day of the wedding. However, Ellen spontaneously decided she would rather have the blue and purple arrangement. She told Sean her intuition told these were the flowers her bridesmaids were *meant* to carry. At first Sean exhibited a rarely seen calm demeanor, suggesting they have the florist order the original bouquets. He cited websites that driveled about how much the flower selection effects the venue, the outfits, and so on. Ellen knew Sean's objection had nothing to do with the slight clash the blue-purple mix would cause, and everything to do with his initial decision not coming to fruition. He had studied the articles that advised on a perfect wedding, approaching the event like a math project. Almost always, Sean was more calculating about things than plain human, and he afforded no space to inexplicable reasonings. Mostly Ellen tolerated this in Sean, but she refused to be completely flattened by that lifeless perspective. Based on defiance more than anything, Ellen told him she was absolutely keeping the new flower arrangements. This contradiction made Sean livid. He belittled her tendencies to go with gut-feelings, and claimed her attempt to *defy their plans* was intentional. Ellen argued the validity of going with the flow, especially over something as trivial, in her mind, as flowers. Sean declared her opinion as nonsense. In the end, there was no reconciling for them that night. Sean stormed out of the apartment to grab a drink. Ellen grabbed her overnight bag and took the car, which was already mostly packed for the camping trip, and left for the woods alone. At the time, Ellen believed she was making a statement of her independence: She could be fine without him under any circumstances.

None of that mattered now. Ellen was alone, with no one to rely on even if she wanted.

She stepped out of her tent with a forced confidence and surveyed the surrounding area. Still nothing to be seen.

She stepped cautiously towards the tree line. Half expecting to discover something like enormous hoof-like prints imbedded in the cold dirt, Ellen was puzzled to find no sign of wildlife at all. No small animals running around, no owls hooting. She felt certain that first disruptive noise had been very close. But, there was no evidence of anything coming close to the tent.

  A mild gust of wind blew by, making the night feel even colder. Ellen looked down towards her feet, regretting not taking the time out to put on a layer of leg warmers. Suddenly the wailing came once more, louder but seemingly even more distant, distracting Ellen from the frozen night air. Without hesitation Ellen stepped into the woods, pursuing whatever was out there. She knew it was ludicrous to do so from the start, but she could not stop herself. Curiosity had control for the moment, pulling Ellen according to its will.

As she ventured further in, a more logical side of Ellen was compelled to examine the situation objectively. It questioned what she hoped to accomplish rushing alone into a wintry forest, chasing a disembodied noise; there was only the slimmest of chances this all would unfold favorably. Ellen's conscious implored her to cease this course, and to return to the assumed safety of her tent. Her legs refused to stop though. Making it this far unharmed, her brave spirit wanted to keep going. Besides, at this point

Ellen still saw no signs of life. Ergo, she felt there was no reason to turn back yet.

She walked for several minutes, but found nothing of the phantom creature. Pushing passed tree after tree, the beam of the flashlight darting left and right too wildly to specify a path, Ellen's imagination began to fill-in the ambient darkness. She guessed what Sean might say about this sequence of events. He would probably call the act inane and perilous. He would have never investigated strangeness like this. He was not adventurous, and obstinately satisfied accepting what was in front of him all there was to life. Offensively sometimes, too. Whenever Ellen had the urge to merely theorize on something fantastical, Sean would refuse to hear her out. His responses started as mockery, but could often escalate to shaming or insults on her intelligence, as he had with the bouquet incident. Ellen's ideas, and indeed her feelings, seemed paltry to Sean's own judgement. His quickness to dismiss and disparage always made her feel small. Every time though, Ellen did as her mother instructed, to hide those hurt feelings, lest they elicit further embarrassment.

Much time passed in the woods with Ellen lost in grief over Sean, she had not realized the wailing ceased. She had been walking completely directionless for an indeterminable amount of time. Stopping for a moment, Ellen directed the flashlight around, trying to find where the noise went. She looked behind her, annoyed for not leaving the electric lamp lit by the tent to guide her back. There was nothing to be seen any direction except for bare trees. Ellen knelt and powered off the flashlight, thinking the light might have scared off the phantom creature. She hoped to trick the phantom into thinking it was alone, so it might make its noises again.

    Immersed in absolute darkness, shivering from the bitter cold, Ellen's fanciful tendencies overwrote her patience to wait and listen. Her mind wandered as hastily and desultorily as her body before. At first, she wondered what the phantom creature may look like, trying to conceive it as something unknown. Her thoughts curved sharply back to familiar avenues though. She envisioned Sean yelling at her to quit daydreaming about things that *do not exist*. Ellen questioned if that was really the only way she viewed her fiancé, as someone so crude and discouraging. To believe that was true made her nauseous and tense. She took a breath to relax, and tried envisioning him being positive. In that scenario, he sweetly pleaded for her to return to the safety of the tent. Even then, Ellen groaned over the absence of his support to continue with the adventure. How the two of them had gotten this far, on the approach of marriage, was becoming painfully absurd to Ellen.

An epiphany occurred to Ellen that their whole relationship could be boiled down to one word: Security. Not in the vein that they felt content and grounded, or even particularly happy with each other. But rather what they formed together was security from the pressures of family and friends, of society in general, to partner up with someone. Meet someone, get married, have kids; otherwise, you will be subjected to constant pestering to fit the paradigm. Really, Ellen and Sean did not complement each other well as a couple. Certainly not enough to pledge their devotion *forever* in front of a gathering of witnesses. Actually, they had little in common. What Ellen and Sean did have in common was upper-middle class roots, and they grew up in the same neighborhood. They knew each other up through high school, and were genuinely friendly towards each other. But each chose different colleges and fell out of touch, as most people tend to as they mature. Besides those initial, miniscule shared elements, their desires were virtual opposites. It was not until a year after college that Ellen would even see Sean again.

Her parents and his were acquaintances. A few times a year, the two adult couples would host a joint party, bringing their individual clusters of friends together. Ellen's mother badgered her into attending their autumn gathering, where Sean's mother seemed all too eager to re-introduce the two. Neither Sean nor Ellen was enjoying themselves that evening, and made jokes amongst themselves about the situation. Everyone around them just expected that was the beginning of a relationship and would not let up until the supposed couple molded from the pressure. Truth be told, Ellen was indeed attracted to Sean for a short while, and had fun dating him for a bit. By the time that glossy picture had dulled, Ellen unconsciously assumed stay with him. She would look around at her friends, and at her own parents, and noticed none of them appeared particularly happy, and figure that was the course relationships ran. In the unhappiness moments with Sean, her parents and friends seemed to be the most forceful about staying with him. Like they wanted her to break, be as divided as they were.

But the signs that Sean was not meant for her were becoming too blaring to look beyond. In the bigger picture, the idea of them being wed seemed as ludicrous as chasing phantoms in the woods.

Ellen could not find a solution passed this revelation, not one to please all parties at least. Returning home to makeup with Sean would solve nothing. In all likelihood, this fight was going to be the end for their relationship. A relationship so laughably weak it could be cut to shreds by flowers.

Time disintegrated for Ellen while she knelt on the frigid ground. She could not estimate how long she had been there. For certain, the mysterious wailing had stopped. There had been no sound from the phantom beast since Ellen moved passed the tree line. She gave one final look around with the flashlight and listened attentively. Nothing. She figured whatever had made those noises must have found a place to settle down. Ellen stood up and turned around, wondering how to head back to the tent. Having entered the woods on adrenaline, Ellen could not recall if she walked in a straight line or not. She assumed she whipped one direction then another based on from where she thought the noise was coming. There would be no easy and no precise trail back.

Remaining in woods until day broke though was not an option. The air was too gelid, and indeed it was too dangerous. Even Ellen could admit that now. If there had been snow, she could have traced her own boot impressions back. With a touch of humor, she reflected on how the one thing that had gone her way this weekend was now another handicap.

Ellen started walking back the general way she came, searching for any clue which might initiate a retracing of her steps. As luck would have it, she did find some of the thicker trees familiar enough to approximate a return path. A slow pace towards the campsite was an obvious choice, fore Ellen was not looking to rush around blindly again, risking getting more lost. To distract herself from the cold air, she tried to glance up at the stars whenever possible. Her mind had been preoccupied with thoughts of the fight, she had not allowed any time to partake in one of her favorite camping activities: stargazing.

    By the time she found her tent, Ellen had forgotten all about the phantom creature that consumed her impulses earlier. It simply had escaped her mind. She sat outside her tent and watched the stars, until they surrendered their sparkle to the twilight of the morning sun. She delighted in contemplation of how everything fades in time.

Revolver Anatomy

Flint placed a single bullet in the cylinder of the revolver, and gave the chamber a thorough spin before smacking it back into place. He made eye contact with his buddies, who were his roommates and only two friends, Drew and Al. They sat together at the shoddy folding table of their foul living-kitchen room, amid unwashed dishes and spoiling leftover food. He tried to gauge if either Drew or Al was looking to renege on the dare. The three of them had been friends for twenty years, and could almost read the others' thoughts just by observing the contorting of their facial muscles. At this moment though, there was little visual indication which way their thoughts were leaning. Both their faces were like stone. Based on his own present state of mind though, Flint speculated they were probably so nervous they could barely move. Regardless, neither of them shied away yet, so he pressed forward with the plan.

At an equal distance from each of them, Flint gently set the gun on the table. The door to their rat-nest of an apartment was bolted, the dusty and stained blinds were down and closed. They already called in sick to their pitiful jobs for the next day, so their cheap flip phones were powered off; no chance of any their parents interrupting with their weekly check-in. Also powered off was the out of date computer they shared. They even unplugged the television and gaming systems. They had finished lunch and used the toilet. Truly there was nothing to distract them from lowering their heads and barreling through this thing to the end.

Flint looked at the gun, then at Al; Al looked at Flint, then the gun, then to Drew; Drew looked at the gun for a long time, then at Al and Flint. All of them were swelling with disbelief their choices in life had burned down to this dark endpoint. With no career options, no girlfriends, and no direction, their lives had become so improvident and insignificant that they could not deny it anymore themselves. They could see how low they are now, and their grief had taken on a grim form.

Life had never been a cakewalk for Drew, Al and Flint. From as early as kindergarten they were ridiculed by their classmates for being duds. They were not smart or gifted with some artistic talent, and were humiliatingly clumsy at physical activities like sports and gymnastics. More remarkably, they seemed intrinsically devoid of ambition. Instead of participating in after school activities with their coeds, or meeting new kids at a summer camp,

Al, Drew and Flint stuck exclusively to themselves throughout their adolescence and teens. Thereby diminishing any probable chance of expanding or maturing through socialization. Of course, this type of irregular formation attracted bullies and inspired taunts. The three of them could hardly go somewhere that did not cost a certain degree of harassment. The perpetual teasing notwithstanding, they were willfully ignorant to what was perceived wrong with their situation. They were quite aware of never being invited to parties or asked out on dates, but failed to see a reason. Furthermore, the exclusion simply did not bother them, and they were content with being bubbled off from their contemporaries. Naturally they became inseparable. The boys filled the years of youth by playing videogames and watching bad movies. To a point however that it interfered with social development and education. They barely graduated high school and never even attempted college. What few other loosely knit friends they had made quickly drifted away after high school. By the age of twenty-one, the three of them had no other contacts, apart from their own parents.

They were social pariahs, ostracized for their predilection for virtual experiences over real life; choosing games and movies instead of social events and activities. All of that though, which had been glaringly obvious to everyone else, was entirely lost on Al, Drew and Flint until recently.

    An evening only a few days before to acquirement of the gun, Drew was rummaging through a department store discount bin of movies. Most were the same few titles, and none was something he and the boys had not seen dozens of times already. While Drew continued to dig deeper, desperate to uncover a new film to watch, he heard a woman speak his name. He glanced up to meet eyes with Aubrey Tyler, his one-time and only girlfriend. She and Drew had dated briefly in freshman year. Although, the entire relationship consisted of them watching TV in the dank basement of his mother's house, with Aubrey trying to make conversation only to be shushed by Drew. It lasted shy of two weeks. After the break-up, initiated by Aubrey of course, she was always sweet enough to say hello in the hallways between classes, or whenever they ran into each other outside of school, feeling sorry for him more than anything else. Like everyone though, she fell out of contact with Drew not long after high school graduation. Now, Aubrey appeared to have only refined with age, looking more strikingly lovely to Drew than even back in school. Their unexpected meeting immediately flustered him, as he could hear himself nervously babble out a reply to her greeting. His confidence trembled, and he proceeded to fumble through her inquiries about his wellbeing and situation. She was back in town to visit family, whereas Drew had never left. Her initial expression of pleasantness to see him again receded quickly. Drew's self-assurance wore even thinner when he noticed a child in the seat of her shopping cart. With Aubrey's ageless beauty combined with her air of responsibility and maturity, Drew failed to think of anything impactful to say. He fell silent, and just looked down in shame. Aubrey kindly ended the reunion, finishing with the words "Take care of yourself, Drew."

    Walking to his car, Drew caught his reflection in the rear window of some car. He could see his shirt was half untucked and stained. He noticed for the first time how shaggy his hair was, and that he was comically out of shape.

Furthermore, he lamented over the fact that his only plan the rest of the week was to play videogames. Aubrey's words, *"Take care of yourself,"* resonated in his mind. She could see obviously what he himself was denying: Someone in need of fixing up.

Returning home to the small one-bedroom apartment he shared with Al and Flint – with their three single size beds crammed into the one bedroom – Drew felt dejected. It took a while for Al and Flint to pull themselves away from the television, but Flint eventually asked Drew what the matter was, as he was noticeably glum. Drew, reluctant at first from a fear he would be mocked, told them of the encounter with Aubrey at the store and how it made him feel. As he suspected, Al picked on Drew for a moment. They had always used juvenile humor to supplement the support they should have offered each other; Al expected Drew to pick on him later that night about something else. But, looking Al over and realizing his position was in no way better than his own, Drew decided he had had enough. He pointed out Al's unwashed hair and other unhygienic habits, and commented on Flint's floundering intelligence and non-existent ambition. He labeled the pair of them pathetic losers. This led to an argument between all three of them, ultimately with Flint and Al ultimately accepting Drew's revelation that they were losers.

They turned morose and sat quietly in the living room for a long period. But, on a somewhat bright side, this eventually opened a line for progressive dialog for once. Progressive in the sense they were discussing how they might become better. However, progressive did not last long. In a tender point of their conversation, Drew confessed he recently had suicidal thoughts. A deathly silence hung there in the room after. Drew hastily tried to lighten the sudden sullen mood with humor. He joked that his luck was so bad, he probably would lose Russian roulette with himself if he attempted to act on his morbid thoughts.

This comment sparked a natural, and under normal circumstances friendly, rivalry between the three friends. Al claimed his own luck was worse than Drew's, and Flint cried his was worse still. In an instant Flint, Drew and Al regressed to their immature bickering and baiting, making which one of them having the worst luck a perverse competition. The arguing became grave though, when Flint told Al and Drew he could get ahold of his grandfather's old service revolver. He boasted about sneaking it out of his mother's house, and then they could settle whose luck was truly the worst. Drew teased Flint that he could not be that clever, not considering Flint would make good on his own vaunting. They belittled each other back and forth, until Flint became fed up and left the apartment. When he returned two hours later, he was in possession of a loaded gun.

The friends unwilling to back-off their earlier claims, the taunting and daring only ramped up from that point. Each deriding the others they would not have the guts to even attempt firing the revolver. They provoked each other relentlessly, until they saw no other way to end the fighting. What seemed like a flash to them, these three best friends found themselves sitting at the kitchen table with a gun and a bullet; a manifestation of how cold and dangerous the bond between them had grown. The dare was to pull the trigger on themselves just once. If they all survived, they agreed to shut up and live their lives as they had been so far;

no more concerns about how they were perceived by outsiders. But If any of them died, the two remaining would have to endeavor to change. Al, Drew and Flint all internally knew the whole thing made no sense. By this time, it became a game of who was going to back down first. All of them were frightened of what might happen when the trigger was pulled, but none had the intellectual capacity to stop the insanity gracefully.

Al noticed both his friends were keeping quiet, so he decided to make the initial move. "So..." He began nervously, "who's first?"

No answer.

Al continued, "I mean...I can go, if you guys are too scared."

"I would go, but..." Flint cut in, wanting to seem not afraid, but then found himself at a loss for words. He worried that If he could not think of a plausible reason, he might actually have to go first. He suddenly leapt to say "It was Drew's idea, he should go first."

'Good work!' Al thought to himself with relief.

'Damn it!' Drew cursed himself. He needed to ricochet the attention immediately, but his mind was drawing a blank. This dilemma indeed spawned from something he said. Although, Drew now found the resolution entirely ridiculous, and was wishing he had kept

his mouth shut. He had led them all down this ill-conceived dare.

Dares came and went around the apartment like farts in the wind, most if not all of them childish and pointless. This one though was a whole new level, and not one they had been naturally gravitating towards. This seemingly impossible scenario was Drew's mishap, and now he was facing a very real chance of pulling the trigger first. The best shot Drew had to draw the aim away from himself was to put Al in his crosshair. "You *really* want to be the one who goes second, *Ally*?"

Al detested being branded as a follower, someone who only did anything after it was proven effective or safe.

Calling him one usually triggered a restive action, to prove he was not. Additionally, a high school bully used to call him Ally, and that aggravated him to no end. Drew used this privileged information to his advantage, expecting to push Al straight for the gun. Only this time, of all times, Al did not react accordingly.

"I'll live with it," Al said with a dry expression. He suspected earlier that one of them might use old name calling tricks to get him to shooting first, and he made a conscious effort to shrug it off when they came. In fact, he dusted off an old insult himself. Giving a slight smile to Drew, "Ladies first, *Drewpy*."

Drew's own high school bully called him Drewpy - like droopy – due to his doughy physique. It was special ammunition Al and Flint reserved for times they really wanted to get under Drew's skin. Neither of them had a body that was better. But, they also did not have names which so easily repurposed into jobs about their figure. It made Drew feel especially loser-like when someone called him Drewpy.

Flint saw this swerving could go around all night, like it usually did. The three of them talked big, but always chickened out when the dare was too dangerous; and this was a new world of crazy. He scolded himself internally for not calling this game *Crazy* out loud, to Al and Drew. Flint wanted now to stand up and shout over them "*Alright guys, let's call it off. It's the stupidest thing we've ever come up with.*" Flint knew however if he were the one to break now, Drew and Al would never let him live it down. Both would have blustered they were prepared to pull the trigger, *if it were not for Flint chickening out*. Which was malarkey. They were not ready to go through with using the revolver, but it would be easy for them to say they would have if Flint became the chicken. Into their old age, all jokes about being a quitter would immediately be linked to Flint. Flint believed he could wait this dare out, but saw no end to the bickering in sight. '*Al already has the reputation for being the most chicken,'* Flint thought, *'he should take one for the team.'* He would try to push Al to quit.

"Al, you have to go first. You didn't pitch in for beers last Sunday." Flint mentally patted himself on the back for remembering that. If reviving old wounds was not going to work, Flint would bet on the guilt trip.

Al got defensive. "You know I get paid different days than you two! I didn't have cash, but you know I'm good for it next Sunday."

Drew saw this was the opportunity to callout Al and get him to go first. He mimicked the sound of a crying baby and pointed at Al's face.

Al turned red with embracement, but he refrained from taking up the gun. Obviously that was what they wanted, and he fought not to give in. If they were going to team up on him now, Al figured the best course was to turn them against each other.

"You know what, why don't you pull the trigger on each other, *then* I'll go."

Al thought to himself *"Nice work."* He was certain neither Drew nor Flint would aim a gun at the other, and so one of them would surely forfeit. After one of them fell, this nonsense would be easier to stop altogether; Al could simply blame it on one of them. He regretted taking any part of this brainless dare. But, he knew he could not be the one to back out first.

However, the plan backfired when Drew shrugged and suggested, "Why don't we pull it on you, and that'll count as your turn?"

Drew looked quite serious. Al worried that Flint and Drew were really considering that as an acceptable option. He never pictured one of them holding a gun to his head until now. Unsettling enough was the mental image that Al began to re-evaluate their friendship. He considered moving out and seeing less of Flint and Drew. That was, if he made it out of this dare alive. Likewise, Flint had never envisioned pointing a gun at either of them before. *"You don't turn a gun on a buddy,"* Flint told himself. *"But if I don't, they'll think I'm soft. Or if I don't fire it at them, they're going to at me."* Flint condemned himself for retrieving the gun from his mother's house, and was cognizant now of what tragedy could be on his hands. If Drew were responsible for how this started, Flint was equally responsible for how it ended. He could not say that out loud though, it might give them the definite edge to make him go first. Unless he aimed it at one of them before that. *"What a mess,"* Flint thought, *'I'm actually going to have to aim this gun at one of my best friends.'*

Flint tapped his fingers on the table.

Drew recognized the tapping as Flint's telltale sign that he was about to make a move. It worried him that meant Flint was really considering pulling the trigger on one of them, or even on himself. This nonsense had gone too far, and Drew came to a decision to end it, consequences be damned. Life had not turned so sour that they could not fix things without this senseless dare.

Al and Flint began to bait each other all over again. Drew took this opportunity, with them both distracted, to jolt forward and grab the gun. He aimed towards the ceiling and pulled the trigger.

A bullet exploded out of the barrel with a near deafening blast. Pieces of the ceiling flew down, as the three of them instinctually shielded their heads with their hands. For a minute they remained frozen in that position of shock and uncertainly, not knowing if one of them had been hit accidently.

They were unharmed, only shaken.

In the heat of everything that had happened that day, Drew had not considered the upstairs neighbor, Linda, until now. He could not recall if he had heard her footsteps above earlier, and so did not know if she had been home. In fact, Drew recognized this as the first time he considered what any of the neighbors might think once they heard a gunshot.

No noises came from above, and Drew figured Linda must not be home. Which was a relief, even if she would certainly call the police when she saw whatever damage was done to her floor. He would much rather explain that to an officer than an injured neighbor; or even worse, a dead friend.

All the gravities that would result from this ridiculous dare began to reveal themselves to Drew's mind. He cursed himself, Al and Flint for being so naïve. He tossed the gun out of the kitchen, away from them three, and stared at the bare table in silence.

None of them said anything.

Al thought to himself, '*My god, Drew is totally a freak. He was going to do it.*'

Flint thought, '*Drew is crazy and I should probably keep my distance for a while.*'

Drew, imagining what Al and Flint must think of him now, was comfortable being perceived as the bad guy in this situation. He participated that absentminded dare and could not change the fact it went where in went for as long as it did. And while each boy played a part along the way, it had started with Drew. He settled for whatever price it cost for being the one who prevented things from going further. He figured that would entail Al and Flint probably labeling him as both crazy and as a chicken, but that was an easy price to pay in the admittance of making a mistake.

Drew took a breath in, indescribably relieved his two best friends were breathing in the same air, and started to cry. Consequence be damned.

Psychogenic Stranger

Since I woke up in the hospital, my wife – if she is really my wife – wants to make every day a celebration. She doesn't go all out, with friends and balloons like a real party, but each day I get a small gift somewhere. It might be a present waiting on the coffee table, or just some random cupcake in between meals. And love notes are left everywhere; short ones, written on those sticky pads. Little reminders that she is happy I'm here. Most people probably would like that sort of treatment. To tell the truth though, it wears thin quickly. Presents lose their effect when you get them every day. Plus, there's a reciprocation expectation to it. Every little present, every tiny love note, I have to exaggerate my appreciation. It's a nice gesture, sure, but after a certain point saying Thank You just becomes a chore.

    I put up with this because Chelsea – my supposed wife – has taken constant care of me as long as I can remember. Literally, since I can remember now.

When I woke up last week, this woman was waiting at the bedside. She seemed stressed and exhausted, like she hadn't slept in days. She sat in a chair with her elbow propped on the bed, nearly on top of my arm, and rubbing her hand against her forehead. When she noticed my eyes were open, she cried joyfully and kissed my hands. I had no clue why. In fact, I couldn't remember much of anything. Even my own name, gone. Believe me, it's scary thing to wake up as no one.

    I kept asking who she was and how I got there. She wouldn't tell me how I came to be in a hospital bed. She just kept saying that *we* were "passed it" and didn't have to think about it ever again. Later, a doctor explained I was in a car accident, but he had few details to give other than no other cars involved. My car had crashed into the side of a building head first. I was alone at the time of the accident, so no one could say what happen to me before that. What they did know was the accident put me in a coma for three days. Apparently, I hit my head real hard, there were some cuts and bruises and my left arm was broken. But the doctor told me I was lucky – he definitely had never been in a car accident, if you ask me.

The doctor said my episodic memory was affected, a retrograde amnesia, and that it may or may never come back.

Episodic memory - as the doctor dumbed down for me - is like recalling visiting the State capital of Illinois, while sematic memory is knowing the capital of Illinois is Springfield. So, personal experience versus generic information. It might seem *lucky* to some that all that base knowledge was still intact. When you take episodic memory away from someone's life though, it means the depth of everything is reduced to zero. Nothing and no one around you holds a personal meaning, no personal experience to connect to. I could remember things existed, like movies and shows or bands, but not what I thought of each one. I couldn't even recall what food I liked, I only knew when I was hungry.

After only a day of observation, I was discharged. The doctor believed my memories could come back with familiar stimuli, like objects around my house.

Outside the hospital, the open world felt unwelcoming. Although, there really was no particular threatening thing giving me that off feeling. Everyone coming in and out of the hospital just looked menacing, the birds perched on tree branches sounded like they were mocking me. I felt so self-conscious, like I would go nuts if I were outside too long. It wasn't debilitating, like agoraphobia or whatever, just an extreme discomfort. The sun was bright in the sky and the air was warm; I had guessed it was early summer, but couldn't recall for sure.

The confusion of the time of year made me feel dizzy. When Chelsea sprinted ahead to open a car door – our car presumably – I rushed to get in the passenger seat. Inside the car, I felt a little better.

    The whole ride home, Chelsea chattered on and on about all the nice things she was going to do for me. I barely listened though, I was distracted. As we got further away from the hospital and closer to home, I got anxious because nothing seemed familiar. Every minute since the doctor told me about the amnesia, I hoped something would snap my memory back. As the sights whipped passed me outside the passenger window, my eyes gathering in dozens of new images, absolutely nothing was jogging my memory. While at the hospital, at least the anxiety of not knowing was limited by the walls. Now though, the anxiety was limited to nothing. Looking out the window as we drove down insignificant suburban streets, every foot further I could see was more I couldn't remember. More uncharted territory I was supposed to think of as old news, as we got closer to a space that should be the ultimate familiarity: Home.

When we got to our supposed home, there was no sudden rush of memories. Nothing. Chelsea almost instantly walked me through all the rooms, asking over and over if I recognized anything. The house felt about as familiar as a hotel room. I had a basic recognition of objects, like lamps and a sofa, but no personal connections to any of it. I didn't recognize anything as mine. It felt like a guest being ushered around a strange woman's house.

Continuing to explore into the night, we examined specific things she claimed were important in one way or another. China dishes we supposedly got from her mother as a wedding gift. Decorative plates she claimed we bought on vacation together. Stuff like that. A few times she left me alone to wander, let me find things on my own I guess, to see if something specific attracted my attention. That didn't help either though. I was just lost and couldn't focus.

We ordered pizza for dinner and drank some beer. The mix of them was delightful. I couldn't have said if that was my favorite brands of either beer or pizza, but consuming both at once sent a sensation down me like electricity. This was the first time I'd smiled since waking up. There's nothing really so unique about loving pizza and beer, but it gave Chelsea and me hope everything would come back. We went to bed early, hoping a long night's sleep and waking up in my own bed would trigger something.

But, it didn't. For a few seconds at first, I couldn't remember *anything* again, like where I was and how I'd gotten there. Then the past few days came back to me, what little time I could remember returned. But that was all I could remember. The rest of the morning was more of the same vagueness as before.

The confusion of my surroundings at Chelsea's home made me frustrated. At least at the hospital everything made sense. A hospital room is a hospital room in any state of mind; you're there because something's wrong and you're trying to fix it, so it's pretty barebones. All over Chelsea's house were pictures, books, figurines, etc. All of which I had no idea what to think of. I didn't know which things, if any, we'd picked out together or why. Everything seemed so polished and clean, like it was never touched. I thought maybe we weren't allowed to touch our own things. More than that, nothing in the place was appealing. The patterns of the bedspread and living room curtains, the artwork in the halls and color scheme of the kitchen, the rugs and the glassware, it was all cheap and tired. The whole house looked like a damn department store catalog. It felt fake and made my head spin when I imagined choosing to decorate like this.

I sat in the dining room while Chelsea made lunch. My head in my hands, I silently wished this was all a bad dream, that I was still in the coma or something like that back at the hospital. Chelsea came in and asked a harmless question, really nothing bothersome, but I started yelling for her to leave me alone. Shaken by the outburst, she rushed out of the room, her eyes tearing up. I felt bad, but didn't go after her. I wanted answers, context, but she didn't have it. Later, Chelsea insisted it isn't like me to become angry and shout, and asked what had gotten into me. She just somehow didn't understand my memory was gone, and I was now a blank slate. I had no past experiences to call on for how to react, or how to control the emotion I was feeling. I tried to explain I was under a lot of pressure. She said she understood, but, in my mind, I didn't care if she did or not. We decided to forget about the blowup, and ate lunch in the living room with the TV on to gloss over our silence.

Then Chelsea wanted to take me for a walk around the neighborhood. These attempts to jumpstart the memories began to feel useless. Sure, it had only been a few days, but there was a feeling of everything being fake or wrong. I desperately wanted to understand why, and the hours that passed when I didn't know felt like weeks. I really didn't feel like going for the walk, but it seemed easier than to argue with her, and a whole lot better than just sitting around the house.

As expected, nothing shook my memories loose. I figured if any memories were going to resurface, they would do so randomly.

Chelsea cooked Salisbury steak with a side of garlic mash potatoes that night, because, according to her, it's my favorite meal. However, I hated it the second it hit my tongue. The sauce tasted sour and felt gooey, and the meat was thin and tough. Instinctively I spit it out and made a gag sound. Chelsea looked shocked and saddened, again. So, I made up something about thinking there was a bug in my food during that first bite, and then forced myself to eat the damn steak. She was being so caring, I couldn't stand to see her down. She shouldn't be punished for my frustrations. The whole time though, I kept thinking to myself there was no way Salisbury steak is my favorite meal.

After dinner, I told Chelsea I just wanted to watch TV and unwind before bed. Chelsea put on some show she claimed was my favorite. But, it was boring and obvious. It was a sketch comedy show, with bad acting, corny jokes, and canned laughter. Nothing about it even make me smile. Meanwhile, Chelsea cracked up at almost every joke. Clearly it was a show she enjoyed more than I did. How she could claim it was my favorite seemed strange. Afterwards, we watched a romantic comedy movie Chelsea said I liked. But, I felt the same way about it. It didn't seem right to me that losing my memory would affect what I found funny or not.

That was when suspicion began in my mind.

That night I laid awake in bed, long after Chelsea fell asleep. I didn't tell her what I was thinking while watching TV, so naturally it wasn't keeping her up like it was me. I just kept going over how she said those shows were *my* favorites, and that food was *my* favorite. I had such a strong distaste for them. When you have amnesia, I don't think that includes losing your taste in things, like humor. Sure, it might seem like a small thing, but when you have no memory small things can occupy your mind. I looked over to Chelsea and wondered if she were lying to me. And if so, for what reason.

In the morning, Chelsea went out to run errands. She wanted me to go with, but I convinced her it might be good for me to be alone for a bit. While she was gone, I went through the CDs in the living room, where the stereo was. There were only a few, and they were mostly easy listening or vocal jazz. Frank Sinatra and Elle Fitzgerald, that kind of thing. I took a minute to reflect thankfully that I still knew how to operate our CD player, and that I could tell a genre of music by the artist. I skipped around on each album quickly. Nothing sounded good to me. In fact, every album sounded trite and sterile. It seemed to me, this is the kind of music you buy when you want people to think you have class. It felt phony. Or, worse, stagnant.

As the last song of an album played out, I began inspecting the few books on the bookshelf above the stereo. There were just three rows. There were two copies of the bible and a few hymn books. The rest were basic classics. Stories anyone would know. Again, I felt the way I did about the CD collection. I couldn't tell if we read these, or if it was we wanted to give others the impression we were readers.

Everything about the house started to feel like a model home. That suspicion in me started to grow, that some part of my story was being left out. There was something big Chelsea was not telling me. My mind even went to extreme scenarios. Such as I'd been kidnapped and she was trying to convince me we were married.

When Chelsea got home from her running around, that's when the little presents started. She brought home a new model car set for me to work on. There were several finished ones in the living room, which Chelsea told me I had put together. They were mostly of vintage models, but there were two modern types. The kit she brought home was for a 1923 Ford T-Bucket hot rod. It absolutely was a fun looking car, and I did have an instinctual urge to start assembling the model. Finally, a moment in this house that felt authentic to me. I had wanted to find a kind way to mention my suspicions, but after she brought me such a thoughtful gift, I decided to hold-off a bit. Maybe I just needed more time.

Later that night we again watched shows she claimed I enjoyed and ate a meal I supposedly liked, which actually I found terrible. I started to become so confused on what to do or say while Chelsea was around.

The next day Chelsea went back to work. She managed a small art and crafts shop. According to her, it was open Monday through Saturday. It was Thursday though, and I found it odd she would go back now, instead of waiting until Monday. Supposedly, she had arranged with my employer to give me more time before coming back. When that conversation took place between them, I had no clue. I didn't even remember what I did for a living. Chelsea told me I was an accountant for a small law practice, and that I didn't like my job much anyway. While she was at work, I inspected the evidence of us as a married couple. We had wedding photos, which would be a difficult thing to fabricate. I brought one of the photos into the bathroom, and held it next to my face while I stared into the mirror. I forced a smile, the kind of false smile you might give someone on the bus who insists on making pleasantries. Then I tried to give a genuine smile, by thinking of something funny. The two variations of my smile looked close enough, but I could tell the slight difference between them. It's in the eyes; they arch more when it's genuine. In the wedding photos, my smile looked more like the false one than genuine. Chelsea's smile was so brilliant and warm, though. It'd be hard to believe that day wasn't the happiest she'd ever been. I couldn't shake the question from my brain of why my enthusiasm didn't match hers. What was I hiding on that day, and am I hiding it still? Or maybe I just don't like having photos taken of me? I could honestly say at that moment I didn't want a camera anywhere near me. I was in a fragile state, though.

    In the dinning room there is a display cabinet filled with glassware. The middle shelf has two wine glasses with hers and my initials, and the date of January 1, 2007. Who gets married on New Years day? Those would also be a hard thing to fake, or too much a coincidence to be someone else's initials. I took one of the glasses out, as if holding it would prove one way or the other. Suddenly, I had a flash of me holding this glass in a banquet hall. In this memory, I'm raising it to make a toast. It was the first real memory that came back. I should have been ecstatic, but instead there was an empty feeling in my stomach. I put the wine glass back, and went down in the basement to search more.

    Downstairs were a lot of boxes, which were marked with my name. Inside one of the boxes were some old baseball clothes and a catcher's mitt. I couldn't quite remember if I played or just collected this stuff, but suddenly I did recall loving baseball. I chuckled to myself, wondering if there was a game on now that I could watch.

Back upstairs in the living room, I couldn't find a baseball game on. I just channel surfed, gauging my reactions to whatever came on the screen. There were good and bad reactions, and I started to learn a bit more about myself. Nothing solid though.

I had lost track of time, and the next thing I knew Chelsea was walking through the door. She noticed the wedding album out, and decided to go back through the photos with me. I asked if something had gone wrong before the wedding or something, but Chelsea gave me a confused expression. She said the day was perfect. She kept saying so as we went through the album, repeating it was perfect like she was trying to convince one of us.

    The rest of the night was typical: A bad tasting meal, followed with bad television. Part of me wondered if I'd always hated her cooking but never said anything. Another part of me started to wonder again if Chelsea was lying. I really couldn't say what purpose she would have for doing so.

    That night was the first time we had sex since I'd come home. It was awkward. There was a basic arousal in me over the prospect of sex, but nothing Chelsea did really turned me on. Chelsea is an attractive woman and a sweet person. But every time the moment prompted me to be aggressive, she made a comment that it wasn't like me. A little dirty talk instinctively came out of me, but Chelsea stopped and made it out to be unacceptable. It felt natural to me. Meanwhile, she did nothing. Had we really always performed in this manner? Afterwards, I could tell it took her a bit longer to fall asleep than it had the past few nights. I'm sure she was questioning the change in me, as I was myself.

The next day was about the same. Chelsea worked, I walked around the house, looking for some way to remember everything. Occasionally passing a love note she'd left somewhere. Chelsea came home. We ate, watched TV, tried awkward sex again.

When we woke up early on Saturday, I was thrown off when Chelsea said something about going to Church the next day. Apparently, we are Christians. Catholics to be precise. This wasn't exactly a shock, as we did own two bibles. But, I didn't know we were routine church goers. I attended mass upon her request. She held my hand the whole time, squeezing hard when specific quotes from the bible were spoken, or during the prayers. After the service ended I knew in my heart I didn't believe in the words of the minister's sermon, nor in the story of Christ. There is nothing wrong with it, I didn't feel animosity towards

Christians. I just felt inside the religion wasn't for me. We went out for lunch before going home. I started working on the new model she had bought me.

We ate dinner, watched TV, and went to bed.

Chelsea went back to work the next morning, but I still had that week off. I didn't know how I was going to get through the week with the routine I'd been keeping. We were down to one car because of the accident, which Chelsea needed. I considered going for a long walk, but had this strange fear that I'd forget the way back. Everyone has a cellphone nowadays. Suddenly I wondered where mine was. If I did get lost, I could always call Chelsea. But without one, I'd be screwed. Not only now did I feel confused, I felt trapped too. I wondered if mine had been destroyed in the car crash. That would make sense.

Pieces of the story were missing. Like, why hadn't any of my friends called to check on me since the accident? Elements that might shed more light on my situation. Were they being kept from me on purpose, or was Chelsea being protective and reintroducing these things slowly? Maybe I didn't have friends. Then, did I not really have a job either? Clearly, I loved baseball. So why was that stuff packed away? Did something happen to where I couldn't face the game anymore? If that were true, having no friend and nothing to do all day, what was the point of living? Nothing against

Chelsea, but what else had meaning in my life? I was starting to get paranoid.

I am starting to wonder if I drove my car into that wall on purpose. If that's true, then I failed at what I wanted to accomplish. Maybe that failure has defined my whole life.

Out of Context

Before she retired to her own hotel room for the night, Vincent's tour manager Stephanie asked if he needed anything else. Vincent failed to deliver any manner of response. Not that it was his intention to be rude or detached, but the gig that night had been particularly burdensome. Everything about the tour had become so, due to the ongoing blowback from his regrettable interview with *Equalizer Magazine* months prior. Since that incident Vincent frequently fell into stupors, where even the people closest to him, as Stephanie was, felt so far away they might as well be echoes in his imagination. Long periods of time became a common thing for Vincent to let come and go before he would answer any inquiry, no matter how minor, almost like an insurance policy against saying something damaging to his reputation again. He sat on his hotel bed, carefully collecting his thoughts to string together a reply for Stephanie. Indeed, he did need something. He needed her to stay, just to keep him company. The past few months had crawled by under an overtone of abandonment, with no link back to Vincent's roots or current array of associates. Stephanie was the last withering connection that had not broken fully. Although, their relationship had splintered. By the time he formulated the right syntax to tell her this though, she had already left the room. He had waited too long to speak up and so now was alone. Alone, with only his waning opportunities and options.

 Up until a few months before this, Vincent was enjoying the benefits that came with rising success in the music industry. Albeit on an independent label, he was now a signed musician, a professional. He was solo, experimental-ambient artist touring with a notable veteran band on the same label, promoting his official debut album.

All the creative credit, all the per diem and the cash from merch sales was his to claim. He burned some bridges and stepped on some toes to get where he was: Old bandmates, (ex-)girlfriends, and even some family members. They were left behind in the exhaust of faces if Vincent believed they were standing in his way. Some of these people might forgive him later and some would not, but all in all Vincent was finding it a fair trade. Mostly, they were easily forgotten when it meant going pro in a field he loved, instead of being stunted in a series of dead-end jobs. However, there were some close friends he retained on his way up. Stephanie, for one. The two of them met in junior high, so had known each other nearly half their lives. Stephanie had always possessed a better adept mind for administrations than Vincent. When it came time to set out on tour, he convinced the label to let Stephanie take the position of tour manager.

Around the middle of the tour, *Equalizer Magazine* sent a press query to Vincent's agent about an interview. Vincent was more than happy to oblige. Smaller publications covered him previously, but *Equalizer* was a reputable webzine read by thousands nationwide. Vincent's agent and tour manager sorted out the arrangements, and the interview was scheduled for an already packed date. Vincent was booked for an in-store performance at an independent record shop, with a venue gig later on, and the interview was to be in between. On that day, Vincent spent some time after the in-store sniffing out connections to satisfy a recreational drug habit; he usually smoked a little pot after a show to wind down. After obtaining some weed from a clerk at the record store, Vincent returned to his hotel to write some new riffs and wait for the interview. Although he typically was relaxed about publicity, he began to feel nervous as time inched closer to the interview ahead. Whatever he said in *Equalizer Magazine* would be read by more people than he had ever reached before. The idea of such widespread exposure instituted an anchoring sense of pressure to his confidence. After some self-debating, Vincent decided smoking-up beforehand might be beneficial. He figured it would push his mind away from the demanding scene and relax him for the questions. He estimated the fuzzy effects would wear off before his set later that evening.

Vincent took a few hits off what turned out to be very potent weed, and lounged around his hotel room, listening to a new CD he picked up from the store earlier.

Spacing out on the bed to the music, Vincent was confused when Stephanie came in and asked if he was ready. He only stared back at her blankly. With a curious tone, Stephanie reminded him that the *Equalizer* interview was scheduled for that day, and the journalist had arrived. Vincent suddenly became cognizant of what was going on, but still felt blindsided when Stephanie escorted an unfamiliar girl through the door. Stephanie introduced Vincent to the journalist, and he stood up clumsily to greet her. He forgot her name instantly. Fumbling his welcoming, mixing up words and sounding like an emptyheaded fool, he started apologizing profusely. Stephanie gave him a riled expression as she pulled a seat to the far side of the room, where she would sit to make sure the interview would finish on time. Facing a major opportunity with a cloudy mind, Vincent wanted to get this over and behind him. He moved to a lounge chair by the window, while the journalist pulled over the desk chair to be across from him.

The journalist introduced herself, again, but like before the name quickly escaped Vincent's brain. He decided to just refer to her as "Miss" for the rest of time she was there. A muffled noise came from her mouth, followed a few seconds later by a concerned expression. There was a moment of silence between them before Vincent realized the journalist just asked her first question. Instead of having her repeat it, he answered "Yes" to whatever the question was, as he wondered how any strand of pot could have this heavy of effect at such a small dose. About the clearest thing in the room to Vincent now was Stephanie's growing aggravated grimace, responding to his erratic behavior. Thinking her judgement removed from the room would allow him to loosen up, he requested she get him a glass of iced tea. Reluctantly, Stephanie did as asked, and left the room to seek out the drink. Vincent immediately felt relaxed once again, and had the interviewer proceed.

Despite some lapses in memory brought on by the drug, and a frequentness to ask for questions to be repeated, the interview felt like it was going well. So long as Vincent could concentrate during each question, a seemingly fluent answer came from him. He told himself that she, being a music journalist, probably expected him to be stoned and was used to this sort of interaction.

At some point Vincent's attention was drawn away by some rapid movement outside the window. A squirrel had jumped from a tree to the windowsill and stared intently inside, which Vincent found quite amusing. Leaning closer to the window slowly, away from the interviewer, Vincent could not stop himself from speculating what the rodent could be thinking right then. During this time, the journalist asked another question. Becoming concerned he would come off duncical for all the times he asked the journalist to repeat herself, Vincent tried to recall the question on his own. Something came to his mind like 'Do you believe women can become Chefs?' To which Vincent quickly answered, "Oh yeah, a woman's place is in a kitchen."

There was an extended uncomfortable silence.

Vincent turned back to the journalist, intending to clarify that he did not believe gender dictated the expected quality of a Chef, and there was no place in modern society to assume men and woman cannot be equally skilled in any position. But, while he floundered through his explanation, an exceptionally disarming expression consumed the journalist's face. She appeared caught in a mix of angered *I cannot believe you just said that* and a disbelieving *Excuse me, would you repeat that?* The uncomfortable silence which came from his comment persisted. Then the journalist hastily packed up her voice recorder and notepad and said, "I think I have everything I need." She obligatorily thanked him and rushed out the door, just as Stephanie came back in with the iced tea.

"That was quick," Stephanie remarked. "She wasn't even here ten minutes."

Vincent was relieved that it was over. He grabbed for his guitar to resume writing new music, forgetting what had just happened entirely.

Stephanie muted the strings on the instrument with her hand and brought her head down to make eye contact with Vincent. "What the Hell were you doing back there?"

Furrowing his brow and shrugging at her, Vincent did not understand what she was referring to exactly.

Stephanie clarified, "You were high during that interview. I've told you, you're weird when you're high. That was a big deal, Equalizer could be a huge boost for you. But you were acting weird, and that might be all she writes."

Vincent shrugged it off. He confessed to Stephanie that he smoked a little beforehand. They argued for a bit over his choice to do so, ending with Stephanie leaving the room in the middle of it, as Vincent kept getting lost in the conversation. After she was gone, he resumed playing his guitar, thinking she was overreacting.

Everything normalized after that for the time.

The following week however, Vincent's touring experience became vastly different from how it began. Even though he was just the opening act, up to this point the crowd had cheered loudly for his performance, girls waited near the tour bus to meet him, and generally everyone on all ends were pleasant to deal with. All of that curtailed instantly. Suddenly no fans attempted to see him, and only a few employees at the venues were cordial. The band he was touring with did not chat much anymore, and the applause during his set dwindled. Even Stephanie started ducking him whenever she could, fabricating tasks to occupy herself. Vincent figured it was only a hiccup in the tour, his fame settling down for a bit, and so gave it little concern.

That cold shoulder continued as the tour pressed on though, to a point Vincent sometimes had difficulty finding out what time he was supposed to be on stage. Even fewer people interacted with him, and the applause dialed down even more.

One day on the tour bus, heading to the next city following a particularly uninspired night, Vincent confronted Stephanie on the recent decline in his popularity. At first, she attempted to dodge the subject with claims of miscellaneous busy work, but Vincent called her out on her newly habitual avoidance. That was when she finally informed him of his distasteful and damaging interview *Equalizer* had published.

Unaware the article had been posted, having naively figured someone would say when it was, he demanded to see it immediately. Stephanie hesitantly pulled the article up on her laptop, and Vincent saw it painted him as dopey male chauvinist. The story revolved around his ill-worded comment about women in the kitchen, only ever venturing off that point shortly to suggest he was barely together enough to forge a full coherent sentence together.

The bad news was not limited to *Equalizer*. Several attacks to his character could be read on other sites in response to the article, agreeing with the negative assessment. Furthermore, Stephanie revealed press calls had flooding in to get a reply from Vincent. She had kept everyone at bay for the time being, attempting to put distance between Vincent and that article. This upset Vincent, as he would rather have had the opportunity to explain himself.

Eventually there was a phone call from the record label to Vincent's agent, with the former talking about going as far as terminating Vincent's contract. Vincent knew he was not yet such a big-ticket star that the label would consider him irreplaceable, nor would his fans find him indispensable; his legacy was only one closed door away from being left in the wind to blow away like discarded trash.

Vincent would not simply roll over though with his head slumped, waiting for the axe to swiftly drop. He ordered his agent to issue a statement that his comments in *Equalizer* were taken out of context, hoping that would open a channel to clear the air. Unexpectedly, that made the public skeptical of his true nature. They questioned whether he was only concerned because he was now under the microscope. There was less an opportunity to clear the air than a chance for journalists, interviewers, and fans to pervert their own version of his original comments. The scene became like a feeding frenzy, vehement with some desire to tear him apart. Vincent, an up-and-coming personality had had a bite taken out of him, and now all the reporters were circling in to the scent of ink in the water.

His agent began to dodge his calls and did only their required minimum. Stephanie became the only person who would hold some sort of conversation, when she was not attempting to ensure he arrived place to place without being harassed by thirsty reporters or angry strangers. She was Vincent's only source for updates, too, and so was the one person left to ask for advice. Stephanie felt there was no quick fix for the shattered image that was now inseparable from his music, and propounded that him quietly staying out of the spotlight for a bit might allow time for the public to forget. By this point Vincent had plenty of time to reflect on everything, and he knew from watching the ebb and flow of other musicians' careers that the public never forgets. They never want to forget the collapse of a young act, no matter what the cause. Overdose, scandal, it did not matter, so long as the story concerned someone who endeavored to reach for the stars but fell for the whole land to witness. Regardless, he followed her advice, believing he got himself in enough trouble already following his own.

Against their hopes, the state of affairs worsened with Vincent's prolonged silence. The absence of his own defense left a void for everyone to twist their own speculations into facts, for everyone else to cut and pasted the portrait of "Vincent, the Misogynist." Apparently, nothing could be done to clear the mud off his reputation.

One afternoon Stephanie came to Vincent's hotel room with a grave expression. He invited her in, and she immediately found a seat before speaking. With a nervous whisper of a tone she reported the label decided to cancel his contract at the end of the tour. The label had called Vincent's agent, who told Stephanie, and they agreed it best he hear it from her – after that, the agent quit. Utilizing their lawyers and convenient, for them, legal loopholes, the label found the power to terminate their agreement ahead of its original date. Without a renewed contract Vincent would be on his own, in debt to the label that had barely started to recoup the advance they gave for his album. There would certainly be no chance of financing new studio recordings himself, and at that time he doubted any significant band would consider playing shows with him. Touring in general seemed like a bad idea.

Ultimately, Vincent was done.

Stephanie, working as both his tour manager and agent now, began searching out other labels that might be interested in picking Vincent up for a new album. Vincent knew though even if there were a label willing to gamble on him, the contract they might pitch would shove him further in the hole.

After weeks of phone calls, Stephanie had no luck securing Vincent with a new contract anywhere. Either they felt he was not big enough, not the right fit, or worst of all they were very familiar with the controversy.

This was the time that Vincent started to feel so dysphoric he could not answer questions in a reasonable amount of time. When he was not on stage performing for an increasingly disinterested audience, Vincent secluded himself in a hotel room or the tour van, where he relentlessly contemplated what rocky roads were in line for his descent. Those limited contracted days were falling off rapidly, and it was only a short matter of time until the serious shellacking which was due would begin. Vincent saw that the details of his future were undefined, but the tone was, beyond doubt, grave. In his mind, he reviewed every misstep on the way up to anticipate what ironic punishment might await him on the way down. He did not know where he might end up working or where he would live, but he knew it would not smell like stardom; It would smell like the ashes of burned bridges.

  The final day of the tour came. Vincent believed the humiliation was not worth the bother of showing up to the gig, but Stephanie convinced him to play his set still. She told him finishing on a limp was better than not finishing at all. Inspired by her resilient ability to look on the bright side of everything and to jog on against unmitigated disaster,

Vincent resolved to end on a strong note. As strong as possible anyway. With his head up, he took the stage in front of an almost non-existent audience, rediscovering the thrill of playing music for the art of it alone, and not worried about the reception.

    Stephanie stood amongst what little crowd there was, instead of waiting just off stage for Vincent to finish so she could try to move him on to the next thing or place. She planted at the center of the floor, right where she always did in the early days, during his first shows at dive venues in their home town. Through the bright lights, Vincent could make her out. He thought it might be her of subtle way of showing he had not lost everything.

At the end of the last song Vincent laid his guitar on the stage and walked off, leaving a final open B note sustaining to fill the venue. The note phased to feedback before the sound crew cut it, effectively ending Vincent's career as a professional musician, now only a myth of which no one would ever speak.

Afterward, Vincent stood in the alley way just outside the exit door of the backstage area. Smoking a cigarette he bummed off a roadie, he watched the anonymous bustle of the various crews inside. Everyone rushing about with their own purposes, functioning in their respective roles of the machine from which Vincent was now extracted. Soon he would be merely another onlooker mixed in the audience, restlessly watching the stage with eagerness for something to happen upon it, trying to get a glimpse of the band behind the curtain.

Against the haze of people in the backstage area, Stephanie stood out as she walked through Vincent's field of vision. She had returned from the main floor and was searching for him, checking everywhere but outside. He marveled in her perpetual dedication. Opportunities had come her way to abandoned ship, but she did not take them. Instead she hung around to the end, and supported Vincent when he needed it the most. Now, when the ride was over, she was looking for him, ready to be told the next move. Vincent knew he could ask Stephanie for anything and she would provide to the best of her ability. He could go back inside and ask her to help him forge a new contract with any label, or to help him figure out a way to go independent. Likewise, he could tell her it was over and that they needed to go back home.

But, while it was true the story was coming to an end for him, Vincent knew Stephanie still had chapters yet to be written. Having displayed herself to be a decent tour manager, it would be irreverent to drag her down when there could be a plethora of other acts that could use her talents and experience.

Suddenly Vincent saw a few nameless stagehands walking with his equipment. Each of them mishandling something in some odd way. He had neglectfully left his instruments on stage, and since no one seemed to be able to find him outside, or maybe did not care to, the staff was ordered by the venue manger to pull everything backstage. Next the venue manger came walking by, huffing about if anyone knew where to find Vincent, visibly upset that he had ditched his stuff on stage. Vincent contemplated walking back inside to take responsibility. But he was already perceived as a jackass and figured no one could think less of him for leaving his gear there; for now, anyway. And if he ultimately decided to leave his stuff there, the club could do with it all what they pleased. It did not matter to Vincent, as the equipment seemed worthless to him at that point in time. Maybe he could sell the instruments for a fair amount, but not enough to even come close to paying back the label. It seemed to Vincent there was nothing left of value at all left in the building.

So he left, in search of a far-off bar, where he aimed to take himself out of context.

Rehabilitated

Non-fiction

I Want the Answers: the untold feminism of the X-Files

Originally published on Chicago Literati

When anyone thinks about the science fiction, suspense television show The X-Files, the thought immediately colligates with its most recognizable character, FBI Special Agent Fox Mulder. Agent Mulder focused his time and energy on the so-called "X-files," Federal investigations that could not be explained by conventional logic and purported paranormal activity. At the beginning of the pilot episode Mulder is given a partner, a supposed helper called FBI Special Agent Dana Scully. The shorthand is Mulder and Scully spent nine seasons and two movies (not counting the return years later) chasing after phantoms and aliens together, with Mulder always identified as the lead character. Which on the surface makes sense; all the explorations stem from Mulder's obsession. Yet, if you step back for a panoramic view, Dana Scully is not just a sidekick. *She* is in fact the lead character, making *The X-Files* more than another science fiction program targeted at a predominately male demographic. *The X-Files* provides an advocacy for feminism in Sci-Fi using Agent Dana Scully as the pivotal character. Essentially, it is her journey that viewers are following along with. Over the course of the series, Fox Mulder's beliefs remain consistent with where they started. He is a flat-line, a foundation. Elements associated with storytelling - change, progress, and investment – come primarily from Dana Scully.

Anything significant to Mulder's character development occurs before the show beings, most notably his belief in his sister Samantha's abduction by extraterrestrials. From beginning to end, few things change in Agent Mulder that would allow the series to move along.

Consider this: Dana Scully was an FBI Agent with a background in Medical Science. It was her astute knowledge in the field that received her nomination to be partnered with Agent Mulder, to provide scientific method and evidence, if any, to the Bureau's X-files. At the time of her assignment Scully was a common skeptic. Like most everyone else at the FBI, she only knew of Fox Mulder by reputation, both for his brilliant work in the Behavioral Science Unit and for his "Spooky" tendencies. So, from the very beginning - in fact even before we are introduced to Mulder - Scully is the changing and developing factor in the story. The day Dana Scully is assigned to a section of the Bureau she never offered serious thought to before is another typical day for Agent Mulder. From that point on, Scully is the one exposed to new viewpoints on the subject of unexplained phenomenon, and in turn is the one who leads viewers into bizarre scenarios. These episodes/cases are not triggering any new emotional reaction for Mulder, especially to the degree they are for Agent Scully. The once ridiculous claims of UFOs and folklores come alive now cannot be simply laughed away for her.

As mentioned above, Agent Scully was originally assigned to the X-files in order to provide whatever scientific evidence possible. Her Division Chief Director hoped her assessments would discredit the X-files so the FBI could shut them down permanently. Several episodes end with Scully typing up a report on that particular case/episode, which she is expected to submit back to a team of Directors at the Bureau. In these reports Scully details whether each case has any scientific validity, whether it should be left opened or be closed, if it remains unexplained or if there is a plausible theory she supports. Ultimately, the X-files lay in balance of Dana Scully's professional opinion. If there is going to be any progress, it has to come with Scully's approval. Of course, in all said episodes Scully judges that the evidence is inconclusive – there would not be much of a show if case after case were closed and disproved. Regardless of how many investigations Dana Scully official claims to be falsely considered paranormal off screen, it means that as enthusiastic and devoted Agent Mulder is to these cases, the effect he has on their outcome, as far as the FBI is concerned, is slim to nihil. Mulder does take it upon himself to investigate on his own, with or without permission to make advancing discoveries, but it is Scully's assessments that allow for him to pursue his leads in the first place. Otherwise the X-files would be shut down and Mulder would be reassigned.

  Towards the start of the second season, Dana Scully was abducted and experimented on; an event which had revenant aftermath. Over the next few seasons she finds a mysterious microchip implanted in her neck, develops a rare and resilient form of cancer, discovers she has been cataloged by a shadow government, and suffers the loss of her sister Melissa when assassins mistakenly terminated her instead of Dana. These circumstances give Agent Scully a more personal investment in the X-files than when she originally was assigned to them. Fox Mulder is notorious for using the line "I want to believe," displaying that he already has decided he thinks there is a truth being concealed. Following the death of her sister, Dana Scully was heard to say "I've heard the truth, Mulder. Now what I want are the answers." Even though Agent Scully remains an open-minded skeptic regarding paranormal explanations, her trust in the Federal Government has been rattled and she suspects what Mulder believes, that there is a massive cover up of something damaging to the public. This is another way Scully leads the audience to an endpoint: Don't believe everything you're told.

      Certainly Agent Mulder's contributions to the story arch cannot be derided. As stated above, he is the foundation for *The X-Files*. But, the truth is without the intervention of Agent Scully his investigations would have wandered in an endless circle, and the X-files would have undoubtedly been abruptly closed down. Scully's presence allowed the show to move beyond its contained environment and to push forward. Does Agent Scully exhibit the value of feminism exhaustively over science fiction? I want to believe.

Exploring the Reoccurring Reincarnation Theme in Wachowski Films

Originally published on Chicago Literati

Every artist has their favorite motifs they apply to the bulk of their work: political or social struggles they perceive to be ongoing, or perhaps emotions they believe are at the root of all scenarios. Native Chicago filmmaking siblings Andy & Lana Wachowski are no exception to this tendency to reuse themes. Virtually every Wachowski production uses reincarnation to effectuate a revolution against oppression. Additionally, Lana & Andy have employed several variations of the reincarnation theory throughout their filmography, to exhibit thorough knowledge of a diverse notion. The relations are sometimes very obvious in their presentation and sometimes not, so let us analyze them independently to connect certain philosophies to specific Wachowski films.

●

The Matrix trilogy

For this epic multiplatform universe, the Wachowskis cultivated philosophical and religious values from around the globe, but leaned heavily on Hinduism for their theme of reincarnation. Hindus believe a soul is formed when it separates from an undifferentiated source, and it will transmigrate during physical death from one body to another, endeavoring to achieve a state of disembodied perfection and exit the cycle of life as we understand it. This process takes many lifetimes and depends on the Karma one obtains during each life cycle. How does any of that relate to a science fiction movie? Neo eventually learns he hosts the sixth reemergence of a code the Machines input to rebalance entropy in the Matrix, by drawing out potential threats to its stability. Neo's predecessors all chose to go along with the program and surrendered their code to be reinserted into the Matrix for a new cycle; what appears to be a noble sacrifice to sustain all life, but truthful condemns humanity to perpetual subjugation. Neo however, now conscious of the plot, rebels and alters his path, which climaxes with a revolution that ends the conflict between Machines and Humans. Learning from and improving upon evident past decisions, The One finds the path of out its cycle.

●

V For Vendetta

True, the Wachowskis did not direct **V For Vendetta**, they only adapted the screenplay. But, their fingerprints are all over it. Here the siblings fashioned the reincarnation theme to fit a Buddhist view. In this movie England sits passively displeased under the thumb of a dictator, who strips away their rights one by one. V, a victim turned vaudevillian vigilante designs a yearlong revolution to influence a citizen uprising, finding his own inspiration from the 17th century "Gunpowder Treason" and its most famous conspirator, Guy Fawkes. Though the political climate differed substantially between Fawkes and

V, the two shared intolerance for tyranny and the decision to take action. The Buddhist position on reincarnation is an impersonal one, whereas no single soul/person is brought back, but their consciousness contributes to an aggregation which new life can be privy to. V was not the literal rebirth of Guy Fawkes, but did claim his ideals. Let's take it one step further. V befriends Evey Hammond, a timid young woman living in fear. Employing deceitful and cruel methodology, V reforms Evey into a brave soul by delivering her his own experiences and viewpoints. So brave in fact that she challenges V on his motives for his revolution. V takes her words to heart and passes the route of the revolution to her, choosing instead to sacrifice himself as a relic of the corruption he has been at odds with. In the end, Evey identifies with V's morals and initiates the final step: blowing up Parliament, just as Guy Fawkes aimed to hundreds of years prior. Through a collective experience and despite the misfortunes that had befallen her, Evey claimed V and Fawkes' ideals for herself. In a closing monolog, Evey declares V represented various people throughout history who all shared the pursuit of justice.

•

Speed Racer

Even the delightfully flashy, psychedelic action flick **Speed Racer** touches on reincarnation to solve a revolution. Although, The Wachowskis took a more superficial approach in this movie, using personal reinvention as a sort of diorama to the concept. Rex Racer was a race car driver, riding under his family's independent ticket. Courted by the conglomerate Royalton Industries to be their representative on the track, Rex refused due to concerns that corporations like such were controlling automobile racing to turn profit. Fearing reprisals against his family when he decides to rebel, Rex Racer faked his own death and reinvented himself as Racer X, a mysterious lone motorist who inexplicably aides Rex's younger brother, Speed Racer, in the effort to expose Royalton Industries and bring the racing business back to an honest state. Rex Racer killed off a persona with too much to lose and adopted a new one free of ties to anything, to affect the next generation of race car drivers towards the demolition of cooperate interference.

●

Cloud Atlas

Gilgul is a Kabbalistic outlook on reincarnation that is shared by certain branches of Judaism. It suggests that every soul brought into this physical world is tasked with certain commandments, called Mitzvot, which must be understood and fulfilled before that soul can ascend to the next realm of existence. Once a body has died the soul is assessed, and if there are still Mitzvot to perfect, the soul is recycled into a new body; which body depends on what Mitzvot are still required. In **Cloud Atlas**, the Wachowskis masterfully impart this philosophy by showing ten characters recycle through time, each exhibiting different degrees of enlightenment. Some grow and advance their understanding, others devolve into pure essence of hostility, and a few stalemate with never learning anything at all. Each of the ten reused actors of **Cloud Atlas** represents different journeys through Gilgul. The revolutions addressed here vary as wide as their cast of characters, but always revolve around oppression of a seemingly arbitrary subculture.

•

Jupiter Ascending

Reincarnation does not presume belief in divinity. Some Atheists theorize a scientific method of the concept. Following death, bodies decompose to subatomic particles. With no physical barrier to contain them, particles become what is called "free radical" and float around seeking new particles to be attracted to. Over a course of time, these free radicals could pull together to form a new person. Over an even larger timeframe, one that consists of innumerable cycles of particle convalescence to deterioration to convalescence, there stands a minuscule possibility those atoms will reunite into previous persons. On that note, the Wachowskis' **Jupiter Ascending** is, scientifically speaking, their most apt depiction of reincarnation. Jupiter Jones, an insignificant house cleaner, discovers she is the genetic reconstruction of an intergalactic royal matriarch, who was a powerhouse of stellar industry. Murdered after undergoing a revelation concerning business ethics, her exact atoms reformed in the exact order thousands upon thousands of years later; only at the bottom of the totem pole. Though here, she assimilates genuine sympathy for the lower-class. Jupiter continues where she left off, and rises back in command to redefine herself and dilute her industrial drive.

●

What we can expect from Andy & Lana Wachowski in the future is undoubtedly more tales that fit their personal trend and movies that inspire forward-thinking. But what, in the end, is the revolution they are striving for themselves?

For a More Just World: an interview with Director Kyzza Terrazas

Originally published on Examiner

Finding inspiration in the world around all of us, Kyzza Terrazas displays a striking talent for projecting his opinions into various, well-constructed outlets. While in Chicago for the Film Festival (his first visit to the city) to screen his first feature length film, **El Lenguaje de los**

Machetes (Machete Language), he paused for Examiner.com to reveal the influences behind the movie, as well as provide an insight to the making of and a little about himself.

Cause and Machete Language
Terrazas cited two influential events for writing and making **Machete Language**, one being the Twin Towers attack in September of 2001 – which happened just a couple of weeks after he'd moved to New York. The other was a few years later in San Salvador Atenco, Mexico. *"The government tried to expropriate these communal lands to build an airport. The campesinos (peasant) there united themselves and created the Front in Defense of the Land. They started opposing this plan and eventually stopped it. One of their symbols was the*

machete. They say it's not a weapon; it's a symbol of strength and a tool they use to work (on the land). I thought that was a very interesting movement, because it talked about the contradictions in Mexico: On one side you have the peasants that are still holding on to their land and their way of life and on the other hand you have globalization. In 2006, or 2005, there was a very horrible repression in that town: The police came in and assaulted, sexually, a lot of women, and they took a lot of people to jail. Some of these heads of the movements were in jail for at least three years. The combination of the two incidences led Terrazas's work to be 'as one which attempted to question the relationship between the political and the personal life, more specifically life as a couple.'

Obstacles and Production

Serving as both the writer and director of this film, Kyzza seemed up to the tasks: *"I think the overwhelming part was just deciding to do it, because it was a project I started thinking about many years before I made it. I never thought this was something another person could do; it felt visceral."* Terrazas perused investors. *"We looked for funds the normal way you do in Mexico and we failed. In Mexico, there are few people who invest in films, because Mexican movies hardly ever make any money. Maybe five years ago, they made a law allowing people or companies to invest ten percent of their taxes. It helps and it didn't. More films are made but not necessarily better ones; it's films that industry wants to see."* Determined, Terrazas pressed forward independently. *"I just decided I had to do it, whatever it cost. So it was done on a hugely small budget, with the help of family and friends. We shot most of the interiors in my grandmother's house."* Kyzza wound up casting two of his friends as the lead protagonists, Ray and Ramona (played by Mexican Punk-Rock star Jessy Bulbo and jack-of-all-trades, Andres Almeida). *"My first idea in approaching Jessy was to ask if she would help us do the music for the band (Ramona's band in the film), and maybe play a smaller character. We did some casting tests and she would read the part of Ramona, and I was struck by her naturality; she was very real. She isn't very much like this character; she is much more cheerful, and sort of playful and happy. I had two options: Her and another, professional actress. I had already cast Andres. It was very clear to me that it was probably not intelligent, on my part, choosing Jessy, since she didn't have any experience, but deep inside I knew she would be better. They (Almeida and Bulbo) had better chemistry."* Picking Andres Almeida was virtually no contest. *"He's a kind of interdisciplinary character. He started as an artist, and in early years he acted in films, and he was also a musician. I knew Jessy before Almeida, but Andres was a close friend, and also one of the first people I wanted to cast. I saw other actors, and none of them were really, at all, what I had in mind."* Apart from the family home, **Machete Language** was shot briefly (2 or 3 days) on land occupied by the **Front in Defense of the Land**, in San Salvador Atenco. *"It wasn't a special occasion. It was more...I had to convince them. I met them through this photographer, who works on a newspaper in Mexico and who covered all of the movements; took pictures from the very early stages to the day of the repression. I wasn't only interested in getting them to let us shoot there – we could have shot that anywhere. I was very interested in what they had to say and knowing them, and just getting know their reality. They were super friendly."*

Past, Present and Future
Before dawning the filmmaker's hat, Terrazas played a number of roles behind the scenes on other projects. Aside

from films altogether, Kyzza has successfully published two volumes of short stories. His latest, <u>Cumbia y Desaparecer</u> (Cumbia and to Disappear) released in 2010, includes concepts dealing with similar subject-matter like **Machete Language**. *"Especially this last book I published. They're not all short stories in the classical way. A lot of them I wrote in this period I'm talking about; feeling a lot of rage and disgust for what was happening."* Kyzza reminisces on and relates his previous releases to more current: *"I felt like I wrote those when I was a kid. And I was – I was nineteen. Back then I think my focus, or my interest, was more with language and creating weird atmospheres. I think back then, I was trying more to look at other worlds; other realities and make stories* out of them. Right now I have the urge that, whatever I do, I have to be honest. What being honest is, it's being self-critical. I don't want to trick anyone into believing I'm something bigger or more than what I am." As Terrazas continues to promote **Machete Language**, he also looks at what's in the future. "Writing is something like...it might be the place where I feel more at home. I want to write a novel someday. I have some film projects as well, some that I'm writing for someone else. I don't see myself as <u>just</u> a director."

About the author

Gari Hart is a Chicago author and musician. This is his first self-published works, and his first collection of short stories.

www.garihart.com

CPSIA information can be obtained
at www.ICGtesting.com
Printed in the USA
BVHW081333270120
570620BV00001B/100